Please help the manatee!

Manatee Moon

Marian Tomsl

Marian Strong Tomblin

Avery Goode-Reid
Publishers

With thanks to Nancy, JoAnne, Barbara and Bonnie.
They're making the world a better place.

I Remember You

Navigating the gentle wave, they swam to the right
When suddenly they saw her, asleep, in the light.

Every little thing is magic, just a heartbeat away
To hold her again—what would she say?

In the sweet territory of silence, Lori slept on
Unaware of the two who, again, were gone.

Rebekah Sawyer

Table of Contents

Lori felt their stares before she heard their whispers. Clutching her books against her chest, she wove her way through the crowded hallway as quickly as the tangle of students would allow. Random sounds became words and, as she neared her destination, the words became sentences. Lori's cheeks grew hot and the hair rose on the back of her neck. Two more doors to go and she would be safe in the chorus room. The doors had never seemed further apart.

"Love your shirt," a tall blonde hissed as Lori passed.

"Nice hair," a short brunette smirked.

Lori counted down the steps. Seven... six... five...

"Where ya going in such a hurry?" The blonde reached out and caught Lori's sleeve. Lori stepped to the right to walk past her. The brunette moved up to block her path. Lori dodged to her left, but the blonde was faster.

"Just let me get by," Lori mumbled to the top of her books.

"Nah." The blonde grinned over Lori's bent head to her friend. "Brenda and me, we want to get to know you better. We want to know more about you." The girl's words were friendly, but her tone was threatening. "And what it's like living with a crazy woman!"

The muscles between Lori's shoulder blades tightened. The familiar, dull aching began.

1

The blonde put her mouth closer to Lori's ear. Her breath stirred Lori's pale brown bangs. "A crazy woman who, I've heard, on nights when the moon is full, is out on the water talking to the fish!" She put her left arm around Lori's trembling shoulders and pulled her closer. "Gotta question for you, 'Lor'. Do the fish ever talk back?"

The first bell rang, and Lori bolted toward the chorus room door.

"See ya after class!" The blonde grinned at Lori's hunched back.

"Ta-ta!" The brunette waved.

The two girls linked arms and sped down the hallway. "Get out of our way," the blonde yelled before slamming into a small underclassman. Papers flew to the ceiling as the boy snatched for his belongings.

"Shoulda been watching where you're going," the brunette sneered.

Lori walked over to the boy and helped him pick up his papers. "Rough crowd." He grimaced as they walked together toward the chorus room.

Lori said nothing and pushed wearily against the heavy door. She had done what she had promised her grandmother and not fought back. Now she was safe. Well, for the next hour.

****

Lori struggled to pay attention to Mr. Stephens as he led the choir through their warm-up. Normally this was her favorite class, and her favorite place to be besides the boathouse at Indian Point Park. Here she could release all her bottled-up emotions while she rehearsed the Christmas cantata. But it was getting harder to concentrate, just like it was getting harder to ignore her grandmother's midnight cruises onto the Halifax River to... to what? To talk to the fish like Bobbie had said?

Lori rubbed her forehead. The lines above her dark brows were pronounced—too pronounced for someone only fourteen years old, but Lori had packed more into those years than most girls her age.

Lori couldn't blame her grandmother for what she did even though it was hard taking the whispering, the staring, and now the outright heckling. The way Mrs. Henderson saw it, the Halifax River held the only clues to what had happened to her daughter and son-in-law, and she was going straight to the source for answers.

All Mrs. Henderson knew—all anybody knew—was that one moonlit night three years ago, Lori's parents, Margo and Jim Sweeney, vanished while fishing off Indian Point. The next morning park rangers discovered the Sweeney's small boat caught in marsh grass with their fishing rods, tackle, and Thermos bottles in a heap in the bottom, soaking wet.

Mrs. Henderson had waved away her friends' words of support as they gathered around her at Mom's Bait and Snack Shack that afternoon. "Margo and Jim will turn up all right," she said, glancing at the white Jeep still parked at the community boat launch. "There's nothing on that river they can't handle."

But apparently there was—the Sweeney's life jackets washed up a week later. The Ormond Beach Police Department never showed the life jackets to the public, and it didn't take long for rumors to start about why they hadn't. When the lifejackets were found, the plastic buckles on the front were still locked firmly together, but the thick straps that had connected the buckles to the vests had been *ripped* from the canvas!

There were no further signs of the Sweeneys. That was why Mrs. Henderson anchored her boat off Indian Point every night the moon was full. Crying angrily for answers from the stars and the sea, she didn't care what drowsy neighbors yelled out their windows to her or how many times the police motioned her back to shore with their high-powered flashlights. Though the officers deposited the shivering woman at her front door with stern warnings that they would press charges the next time they had to bring her home, the men knew they would find Mrs. Henderson out on the Halifax River the same time the next month, and so did she.

What was it like living with a crazy woman, Bobbie had asked. If only she knew how crazy Mrs. Henderson was! Crazy with grief. Crazy because she couldn't put the past peacefully to rest.

"How was school today?" Mrs. Henderson asked as Lori stepped through the rough-sawn door at Mom's Bait and Snack Shack. There were five stools at the counter but only one was occupied. Lori eyed the lone customer. It was Glenda Hayes from up the street. The woman with the shoulder-length frizzy gray hair did not acknowledge Lori, and the girl ignored her. That was the way everybody did since Miss Glenda got out of the mental hospital.

Lori slid onto the furthest barstool and gratefully accepted the steaming plate of homemade onion rings and the icy Coke. She popped the bottle cap off with a quick tug against the rusted opener, and avoided answering her grandmother's question by looking up at the beamed ceiling as if she had nothing else on her mind except seeing the bottom of the clear glass bottle. It wasn't entirely an act—it was a scorcher today. But it always seemed hot in Ormond Beach, Florida.

The bottle was empty; Lori was out of excuses. Mrs. Henderson wasn't someone who used words needlessly—when she asked how you were doing or how your day at school went, she expected answers. "I'm not big on making small talk," she stated bluntly. This endeared her to some, and made her an enemy to others.

"School was fine." Lori squeezed a thin line of ketchup

5

around an onion ring while she debated the best way to continue the conversation. Her grandmother seemed oblivious to the barbs thrown their way. Maybe after another fifty years, after Lori's skin was tanned to the consistency of alligator hide, she, too, could rebuff anything. For now though, the words stuck, the sideways glances stung. "Mr. Stephens says the cantata is coming right along."

Mrs. Henderson straightened proudly. "And your solo?"

"Still has a couple of rough spots, but all in all he seems pleased." Lori smiled shyly, remembering her teacher's words of praise.

Mrs. Henderson wrang out a faded sponge and ran it over the cracked pink Formica counter. "I had problems when your mother wanted to name you after the Lorelei." She paused, remembering. "Never was one for high-falutin' names. Give me a 'Jane' or a 'Nancy' any day."

Lori smiled: her grandmother's name was Nancy Jane Henderson.

"But Margo had her heart set on naming you after the beautiful creatures in those mythology books she was always carrying around. 'We'll name her "Lorelei", Mama, and she'll sing as sweetly as a bird' she said." Mrs. Henderson turned her back abruptly, pretending to hear a customer walk up to the order window. She pulled a thin paper napkin from the pitted chrome dispenser and blew her nose roughly into it. "Allergies," she muttered.

The black Halifax River lapped against the pier. A seagull landed on a piling outside the front door. Lori dropped her empty bottle into the recycling bin. The sharp clinking of glass against glass startled the bird and sent it soaring into the turquoise sky.

The silence was broken by the growl of engines as a sleek white yacht sped down the Intercoastal Waterway. Lori braced herself against the counter and watched the boat's deep, v-shaped wake gain strength as it rolled across the river toward the pier. The first wave slammed into the tiny shack. Spray flew into the air coating everything it touched with a salty film.

"Idiot!" Mrs. Henderson pulled up the hinged countertop and darted out the back door of the bait shack. She ran with slippery steps to the end of the pier. "The sign says 'Idle Speed!'" She shook her fist at the disappearing stern. "This is a no wake zone!"

Her protests were drowned out by a second, even larger motor yacht, traveling north. Mrs. Henderson hurried back to Lori. "Guard those bottles." Lori threw a protective arm across a row of sodas jittering toward the edge of their shelves. Miss Glenda gripped the counter. The three women weathered the man-made storm in silence.

"Some day this place will fall down around my ears," Mrs. Henderson grumbled after the wake had subsided. "Those yachts, throwing their huge wakes, tear everything up! Found some weakened boards yesterday—they won't last long once the bluefish start running and the anglers follow. Someone'll put his foot through sure as shootin' and sue me. And that'll be the end of my business. Which would suit Joe Simpson just fine, wouldn't it?"

She jabbed a plastic bag of fishing tackle back onto its display hook. "Old man Simpson said he'd be over to make repairs, but he's in no hurry—this land's become too valuable for just me and my bait shack. If we were gone, he could sell the property for five times over what I pay him in rent. Except I got a paper that says he's got to keep the building up until my lease runs out." Mrs. Henderson chuckled dryly. "In another nine years!"

Lori shook her head. Nancy Henderson and Joe Simpson had antagonized each other for as long as the girl could remember. The two were a rare breed—both Central Florida natives, both born in tiny Ormond Beach even. Beyond that, however, they might as well have come from opposite sides of the planet.

With his unnaturally black hair and chest full of gold chains, Mr. Simpson fancied himself a ladies man. While pressing his lips to an unfamiliar set of female knuckles, he would introduce himself as "Captain Simpson, Pilot". It wasn't a complete lie—Joe Simpson supplemented his retirement income by pulling advertising banners behind his ultralight airplane. The small craft, outfitted with an inflatable boat hull so it could take off from or land on water, buzzed and swooped over sunbathers like an oversized dragonfly, delighted with its long, colorful tail. During his off hours if he wasn't sunning himself in a disconcertingly small bathing suit on the bow of his cigarette boat *The Love Machine*, old man Simpson could be found prowling city hall, hounding officials with his latest development ideas.

"What Ormond Beach needs to do," he'd say to anyone he could corner, "is catch all the manatees, ship 'em back to the West Indies or where ever it is they came from, and tear down all those stupid no wake signs." He'd then jerk his thumb over at his orange El Camino parked at an angle so that it took up two places in the municipal lot, and

wink at its custom Save the Manatee license plate declaring YUM YUM.

"Or have the world's biggest fish fry. I hear they make good eatin'!"

Mrs. Henderson was fond of saying that if she were to cut a vein, her blood would run as black as the Halifax River. Every evening after closing the bait shack she could be found at the end of the pier listening to shrimp pop or watching mullet leap. At sunset when the surface of the river became still and glassy, she searched for the telltale swirl of a manatee. She cringed whenever boaters sped past the signs declaring the area a protected manatee zone—propellers are razor-sharp against the skin of those creatures swimming just inches beneath the surface.

Lori spent a few more minutes helping her grandmother straighten the store, then climbed on her bicycle. Though she didn't have a particular destination in mind, her body was on autopilot. After peddling south on Beach Street for three blocks, Lori poked the front wheel of her bike into the metal rack at Indian Point and climbed off.

Central Florida was once home to the Timucua Indians. A peaceful, agrarian people, these Native Americans clustered their circular huts along the banks of the Halifax and St. Johns Rivers, and hunted the wildlife there that was plentiful. The Timucuans lived isolated from the rest of the world until the 1700's, when French and Spanish explorers marched through the area in search of gold. The soldiers brought war and disease. By 1750 the Timucuans were extinct; the only evidence of their existence in Ormond Beach was the ancient burial mound rising out of the ground on the corner of South Beach Street and Mound Avenue.

Locals referred to the riverfront property across from the burial mound as Indian Point. The city plan called the same piece of land "The Wm. B. Hayes Memorial Park." It was said that Mr. Hayes, while visiting Florida from St. Louis, Missouri in the 1940's, won Indian Point from a one-armed man in a poker game. It was also said that the one-armed man had won Indian Point in a previous card game, back when he had two arms. Indeed, word was that *all* of Indian Point's owners experienced serious mishap once they claimed the property, and that they *all* passed the land on to someone else as quickly as they could!

Mr. Hayes, a son of the "Show Me" state, scoffed at the notion that mystic Timucuan rituals had tainted the land. He set about building a rambling white farmhouse and filling it with a wife (an out-of-towner oblivious to the legend) and seven daughters.

The years passed. Mrs. Hayes, an aspiring sculptor, spent much of her time creating whimsical creatures in concrete and seashells, and displaying them throughout the estate. One sunny September afternoon Mrs. Hayes and her daughters carted life-sized figures of a manatee and an alligator from the studio. The manatee statue was mounted to a piling beside the boathouse, and the alligator was trucked through the orange grove and settled beside a lily pond. That night Mr. Hayes disappeared while taking a moonlit stroll across the grounds. Though his body was never found, his shirt was pulled from the river, ripped apart at the seams. The community decided an alligator was responsible. A funeral was held. The casket contained only the shirt.

By selling off parcels of land, Widow Hayes was able to support herself and her seven girls. One March evening, oldest daughter Sharon vanished while swimming near the boathouse. Her torn bathing suit washed up the next day. The entire town went alligator hunting. The creature was never found.

Every few years after that a different member of the Hayes family disappeared. By 1974, the entire clan, except youngest daughter Glenda, had succumbed to the monster. Twenty years ago, police were called to the Hayes property by neighbors complaining that Miss Glenda was keeping them awake. Startled officers found the woman wandering fully clothed in the Halifax River searching the muddy bottom with her bare toes. "The

11

door! Where *is* that door?" Was all the hysterical woman would say as the EMT's bandaged her feet, bloody with cuts from oyster shells. An inquest was held the following morning, and Miss Glenda was involuntarily committed to a mental institution.

The trust fund that had paid the property taxes during Miss Glenda's absence was now depleted; the city was preparing to foreclose on the estate. Miss Glenda, recently returned to Ormond Beach, was doing everything she could to delay the proceedings, but developers had great plans for the valuable river front property. "We'll call it 'Indian Pointe' with an 'e'," they chuckled greedily. "And that 'e' is gonna cost plenty!" Joe Simpson lived next door to the park. He was all in favor of the new development—it would increase his own property's value.

The rest of Ormond Beach wanted nothing to do with Indian Point. All that remained of the original estate was the dilapidated home, a small corner of the gardens overgrown to the point of suffocation, and a two-story boathouse perched at the end of a long, rickety pier. The place was considered sinister—"Cursed!" locals whispered as they kept to the opposite side of Beach Street. While other gardens were popular sites for parking parties, lovebirds avoided Indian Point. Stories of shadowy movements, windy whisperings, and laughter cut suddenly short kept the place empty after dark. That was one of the reasons Lori loved it so. People avoided her, too.

Lori's footsteps crunched softly as she followed the crushed oyster shell path winding through the park. She ducked when she passed under Miss Glenda's kitchen window. The woman's car was in the shed, and Lori didn't want to get

caught trespassing. Most kids her age ignored this spot. Younger ones, though, filled their pockets with shells from the parking lot and competed to see who could hit the most statues as they walked by.

Lori paused in the shade of a gnarled orange tree to catch her breath. Perched on a wooden stand in the bamboo across from her was one of Mrs. Hayes' creations—a life-sized concrete owl. Once handsome, the bird was now battle scarred from its years as a target. Its metal toes, freed from their cement skin and exposed to the salty air, had rusted away to flimsy threads; daylight glowed through his remaining yellow glass eye.

Lori swung from a low branch considering the bird for a moment, then let go to find Mrs. Hayes' alligator. There he was, sunning himself by the lily pond as he had for the past half century. The beast grinned benignly up at the girl as his mouth had been picked clean of its seashell "teeth" years ago. The grass around him was beaten down from visitors posing with one foot planted bravely upon his broad back. Mrs. Hayes' whimsies seemed harmless enough in the sunlight.

They turned menacing at sunset.

Lori looked up at the reddening sky. She shrugged. It would be dark soon, but she was more afraid of running into someone made of warm flesh than of cooling cement.

She hurried past the free-flowing spring and a life-sized statue of a Timucuan brave staring into the pool of water at his feet (the odor of rotten eggs from the sulphur water repulsed her. Besides, she needed to get out to the boathouse before it was too dark to cross the crumbling pier safely.)

13

The shell path ended at the foot of the boardwalk. Lori ignored the Keep Out sign and threw her leg over the rusted chain strung between the first two pilings. The boathouse was her favorite part of the park: it was near here that her parents loved to fish, it was near here that their empty boat was discovered.

Lori held onto the handrail as she walked. Most of the boards were cracked, and many of the pilings had settled unevenly causing the pier to tip. She reached the end of the boardwalk and sat down on the last splintery plank. How many hours had she spent here staring out over the river trying to recreate the events of that night? She glanced at the concrete manatee poking his head up from the river beside her. Fifty years of wind and rain had mellowed his frolicsome grin to the patient smile with which he now regarded his watery world.

Something soft brushed against her hand. Lori picked up the orange blossom in surprise—citrus trees had quit blooming months ago. She held the flower up to her nose and filled her lungs with its heady fragrance. Suddenly Lori was eight years old again, picnicking with her parents in the Hayes' grove. Her mother was spreading peanut butter on a piece of bread, her father had just called the girls to come out onto the boardwalk to see the manatees swimming by. The memory, like the scent, was sweet. So sweet it hurt.

Lori crumpled the blossom and threw it away. The flower bounced off the concrete manatee and spun twice in an eddy before being carried off by the current. "I guess it's just you and the fish who know what happened to my folks," Lori said to the manatee statue. The sound of her words startled her—she didn't know she had spoken them aloud.

The top of the river had changed from bright gold to dull bronze. The dimming sun warmed the back of her neck. Lori wedged her chin into the crack between her knees. One tear rolled down her cheek, then another. When she roused herself, the world was black. There was no moon; thick clouds concealed the stars. Lori rose painfully to her feet and began inching her way down the pier.

Crack! Her right foot broke through a board.

I'm just like my grandmother, the girl thought miserably, clinging to the handrail. *Except I expect answers from statues!*

"Ladies and gentlemen, may I introduce *Trichechus manatus latirostris* from the order Sirenia," a man said from the back of the dark classroom. "Elusive and rare, this legendary creature's beauty is said to have lured countless ancient mariners to their doom upon the rocks. Sunstruck seafarers called them sirens or mermaids—" a soft whir and a click brought a refrigerator-sized image of a manatee into view—"we call them the Florida manatee."

The class erupted into laughter. Lori stopped doodling in the margin of her science notebook to look up at the lumpy gray creature floating serenely across the top of the movie screen.

"Well, we think he's beautiful," chuckled Wayne Hartley, a ranger with the Florida Park Service. "Meet Jethro. He's a little guy, only nine feet long and about a thousand pounds."

Lori shook her head. She had a hard time believing anyone could confuse Jethro with Disney's Ariel.

Another whir and click, and Jethro was replaced by a mother manatee nuzzling the small, wrinkled face of her calf. The class greeted the pair with aah's of appreciation.

"This is Dolly and her calf, Holly," Mr. Hartley continued. "Dolly is eleven feet long—that's like two living room sofas

16

put end to end—and a slender 2500 pounds." The class laughed again. "Holly was born this summer. She checked in at a little over three feet and seventy pounds. Holly is lucky to be alive.

"A few years ago, Holly's mother, Dolly, was found hanging out at a marina. Some boaters noticed she was having a hard time swimming so they investigated. They discovered that Dolly had fishing line wrapped around both of her flippers.

"No one could believe what happened next: Instead of backing away like manatees usually do when someone tries to touch them, Dolly floated right over to the men, rolled onto her side, then stuck one flipper up into the air! She stayed still for an entire hour, allowing the boaters to clip the fishing line off of her. When that side was free, Dolly rolled over and held up her other flipper." Mr. Hartley smiled. "It was amazing. Dolly stayed there until she knew the men were finished."

Mr. Hartley moved to the front of the room. He pressed a button, and a map of the United States appeared on the screen.

"Manatees are migratory creatures. As long as the water is warm, they can be found along the coast any where from the Florida Keys on up to Rhode Island; in springs and rivers like the Halifax River where Dolly was rescued; and over in the Gulf of Mexico.

"You'd think that because manatees are covered with fat they can survive cold temperatures, but they can't. Once the water starts cooling they must move into their travel corridors and migrate to warmer waters, or they will die of hypothermia. Blue Spring, where I work, is one of their destinations. Our water temperature is 72 degrees year-round.

"It's imperative that boaters along these travel corridors stay away from the shoreline. Manatees eat and rest in shallow areas, and this may be one reason why boats so frequently hit them. It's not that manatees don't hear boats coming—they can hear sounds up to two hundred feet away—but they're like us in that they can't tell which direction the sound is coming from. So if they're in shallow water, they can't dive quickly or deeply enough to avoid being hit."

Mr. Hartley returned to the slide of the mother manatee and her baby. "Look at Dolly's head. See that crescent-shaped wound? That's from being struck by a boat. Fortunately her injury wasn't fatal, but that's no guarantee she'll survive her next encounter with mankind."

Lori looked back down at her notebook. She didn't want to see the animal's scars: her grandmother belonged to four different wildlife organizations, and Lori was only too familiar with the damage boats could do.

"Your teacher tells me you have a field trip to Blue Spring lined up for January. If it's cold then like it was last year, we should have a lot of manatees in the spring run. Now, are there any questions?"

A girl in the back row raised her hand. "What do they eat?"

The ranger smiled. "Just think of manatees as underwater lawnmowers," he said. "They eat ribbon grass, shoal grass, hydrilla and water lettuce—marine vegetation that would have to be removed using dangerous herbicides if manatees weren't around to keep it under control. A manatee consumes about ten percent of its body weight in aquatic vegetation a day, so an adult like Dolly is kept pretty busy eating her quota of two hundred and fifty pounds. Matter of fact, eating and sleeping are about all she does."

"How do they breathe?" a boy on the front row asked. "Do they have gills like fish? My dad says they can stay under water for a real long time."

"Manatees are mammals, just like you and me," Mr. Hartley replied. "They swim in the water, but they don't breathe it like fish do. Their lungs lie along their backbones and extend two-thirds of the way down their bodies. If your lungs were that big, they'd reach your knees!"

The class laughed.

"So with lungs this large they can stay submerged for two or three minutes at a time while feeding, and for as long as twenty minutes when resting."

"How long do they live?" Lori's teacher asked.

Mr. Hartley arched his eyebrows. "Ah, that's a tricky question. Because manatees eat as many plants as they do, their teeth wear out from all the sand that gets into their mouths. As the older molars in the front of the manatee's jaw wear out, they fall out, and new molars move forward. Some researchers call these teeth the 'Marching Molars.' You know, only one other mammal on earth has this same arrangement. Can anybody guess which one it is?"

The class looked at him blankly.

"The kangaroo! And because of this continuous renewal, manatee teeth are of no use to scientists when guessing the animal's age. One thing we do know for certain is that the South Florida Museum has a mascot named Snooty who's lived there for over fifty years."

Lori's teacher joined the ranger at the front of the class-room. "We're about out of time for today," she explained, "but is there one last bit of information you'd like to leave with the students?"

Mr. Hartley nodded. "There are several organizations dedicated to protecting manatees and they have very informative web sites. Remember though, it is up to you, the boater, to respect the manatee zones. It is up to you, the fisherman, to dispose of your fishing line and litter properly. And finally, it is up to you, as the parents of our future generations, to respect wildlife so that one day *your* children can watch these animals swimming in the wild.

"Take care, and I look forward to seeing everyone at Blue Spring in January."

Lori put her fork down and stole a glance at her grandmother. Mrs. Henderson hadn't touched her food either. This was an anniversary dinner, but not one that they had looked forward to eating. Exactly three years ago tonight Lori's parents had disappeared. Mrs. Henderson looked out the window. "Just like it was back then. Full moon made it bright as day."

Lori remembered: as her parents hugged her goodnight and pecked Mrs. Henderson's cheek, they had admired the sky, lit up as if it were midday rather than midnight.

Her grandmother pushed her chair away from the table. "I'm going out for a while."

Lori didn't have to ask where, she knew. "I'll keep the light on."

Mrs. Henderson didn't acknowledge her. Her mind was already anchored off Indian Point.

Lori scraped the plates and stored the rest of the meal in the refrigerator. They'd get hungry eventually. She stretched out on the sofa and waited for her grandmother to return.

Headlights flashing through the front windows woke the girl. Lori didn't realize she had drifted off. She stumbled sleepily to the front door and opened it before the policeman could ring the bell. "Hello, Officer Barker," she said, stepping aside for him and her grandmother.

"Good evening, Miss Sweeney," the man returned her greeting. The three moved into the kitchen. Lori reached for the coffee maker. "Not tonight, thanks," he said when he noticed what she was doing. "I've got a busy shift ahead of me. You know how the full moon always brings out the loonies!" He glanced at Mrs. Henderson then back at Lori. "I'm sorry."

Lori shrugged: they had become friends over the past three years and, as an officer of the law, George Barker had an obligation to the community to bring the ranting Nancy Henderson home. Lori walked him to the door.

"She seems more upset than usual." Officer Barker nodded over his shoulder toward the kitchen. "Wish I could stay for a while…"

"Yeah, well, she'll be okay." Lori's shoulders sagged. "Thanks for taking such good care of her."

"See you next month." The policeman tipped his hat and walked to his patrol car.

Lori smiled thinly as she shut the door. She went back into the kitchen. It was empty. "Grandmama?" She walked to her grandmother's darkened bedroom and peered in. "Are you in here?"

There was a sharp tug on her sleeve, and Lori found herself in the room with her back pressed against the wall.

"Is he gone?" Mrs. Henderson asked, squeezing Lori's arm with chilled fingers.

Lori nodded in the dark.

The old woman was breathing quickly. Lori felt her shiver. "Grandmama, you're frozen!" She twisted to reach the overhead light switch. Mrs. Henderson released her grip. When Lori turned around, her grandmother was

22

curled up on her bed. The girl got down on her knees and searched the woman's pale face. "Grandmama, what happened?"

"The wind, Lori. The wind. At Indian Point." Mrs. Henderson moaned while the girl pulled the bedspread up over her. "Trying to tell me something... Whispering through the bamboo... In the trees..." The woman's gray head rolled fitfully across her pillow. "*Your name, Lori!*"

Mrs. Henderson sat up, her eyes wild. "It was calling out your name! But it can't have you too," she cried. "I won't let it!"

Lori settled the old woman back down. "Don't worry Grandmama." She adjusted the covers and kissed the frowning forehead lightly. "I'm here. We're fine. You rest."

After a few minutes Mrs. Henderson's eyebrows relaxed. The deep lines etched around her mouth softened. A low *purr* followed the girl to the bedroom door. Lori closed it behind her and walked into the kitchen.

"If the wind wants to talk to me," Lori said, shoving her arms into the sleeves of her windbreaker, "we'll talk!"

Lightning flashed across the tops of the trees as Lori peddled her bike down the driveway. She turned right towards Granada Boulevard. It was well past midnight and no one else was on the street. She was at Indian Point in a matter of minutes.

Her bike tires crunched across the shell parking lot. Lori climbed off but kept one hand on the handlebars. With her free hand she fingered the flashlight in her jacket pocket (it was one thing talking about going to Indian Point while she stood in her grandmother's cheery kitchen, it was another being here, alone, in the middle of the night!)

The street lamp above her was out of order. Lori looked nervously around. Between flashes of lightning, the park was colorless, a mixture of light and shadow. Lori felt like she was standing inside an old black and white TV show. Invisible tree frogs called *reep reep* from the lily pond. *Ba-rum* replied a far-away bullfrog.

A huge, full moon cleared the trees. Now everything was different shades of yellow. Lori's left hand began to ache. She dropped her bike onto the grass and flexed her fingers.

"All right, Indian Point." She jutted her chin skyward.

"You wanted to talk to me? Let's talk!"

The moon disappeared behind a cloud.

The frogs fell silent.

Then it started, behind her, in the bamboo. A gust of wind sent the tall stalks tapping together like chattering teeth. Lori pulled out her flashlight and clicked it on.

"Lori," the leaves whispered.

The girl turned around and waved the beam of light into the bamboo. "Who is it?"

"Lori," repeated the boughs of the orange tree.

She aimed the flashlight upwards. "What do you want?"

"Lori," signed the palms next to the Indian burial mound.

"Talk to me!"

The bamboo called her again.

Then the orange tree.

Then the palms.

"Lor-ee! Lor-ee!" screeched the cicadas in the grass at her feet.

"Lo-or-i!" rumbled the bullfrog.

The words swirled around her and inside her brain. The batteries in her flashlight went dead.

Lori threw the useless light onto the grass and picked up her bike. *I'm going home!* she decided. A quick, loud *Crack!* warned her a split second before *Boom!* a bolt of lightning struck the old orange tree beside her. Lori dropped her bike and fell to her knees, shielding her head from the sparks. A creaking and groaning made her look up. She blinked, trying to focus her eyes.

A heavy limb was falling off the tree. It was going to hit her!

Lori rolled onto the grass. The limb crashed onto the

path in front of her. Now a six-foot wall of leaves blocked her escape to Beach Street.

Lori scrambled to her feet and ran past the stand of bamboo leading to the Hayes' driveway. Long twiggy fingers pulled her hair. Sharp sticks poked savagely at her arms, her legs. Lori's feet slipped out from under her. She fell onto her back, knocking the wind out of her lungs. The stars above her took up a dizzying dance. Lori closed her eyes, willing them to stop. *Stop!* she tried to scream out, but she was choking on her fear. She couldn't breathe!

"Lori!"

The girl squeezed her lids tighter.

"Looori!"

The speaker was very near.

Lori peeked up through her lashes. Mrs. Hayes' concrete owl was directly above her rocking on its wooden perch. Back and forth, back and forth, the bird threw its rigid body. Its one yellow eye glowed wickedly in the moonlight before he launched himself at her head.

Lori flipped onto her stomach and crawled off the path into the underbrush. Smilax clawed at her face as she pushed her way through to the clearing at the lily pond. She rose, trembling, to her feet.

A bullfrog hopped into the pond with a soft *plonk.* Lori leaned over and rested her hands on her knees. She sucked the damp night air shakily into her lungs. Then her breath caught in her throat. She could hear something heavy being dragged across the shell path!

She tried breathing through her nostrils to quiet the pounding in her ears. *One, two Mississippi in; One, two Mississippi out.* She squinted into the shadows. And into the face of Mrs. Hayes' concrete alligator. It was opening its jaws!

Lori couldn't move. It was as if she, too, were made out of concrete. She watched helplessly as the reptile pulled a front leg up and lunge towards her. His deep "Lori!" sent her spinning in a tight, frightened circle.

The path to the boathouse lay to her left. Lori chose it and hurried past the sulfur spring. The Timucuan brave looked up from the pool of water at his feet. He stood and reached for her. "Lori!" She pushed her fingers into her ears. "Leave me alone!"

"Lori?"

The terrified girl skidded on the dewy grass. She recognized *this* voice. "Dad?" She raced to the foot of the boardwalk. "Dad? Daddy, I'm coming, do you hear me?" She threw her leg over the rusty chain. "You and Mom stay where you are! I'm on my way!"

Ignoring the cracked planks, Lori sped headlong down the pier. The hood of her windbreaker caught on a nail. She yanked her arms out of the sleeves and kept running.

The full moon cleared the clouds too late for Lori to see the broken board in front of her. The toe of her tennis shoe caught on it. She tripped, stumbled, then staggered toward the handrail. Her right shoulder broke through the decaying wood.

Lightning flashed as Lori fell into nothingness.

A seagull, dozing atop a barnacled piling, flapped its wings in agitation and flew up onto the boathouse. The sound of Lori thrashing about in the water sent him stomping across the tin roof. "Has anyone bothered checking the time," he squawked over the edge. "Some of us are trying to sleep!"

Lori paused in her panic—the water was shallow enough for her to stand—and called up to the boathouse. "Hello? I'm so glad somebody's there! I, I feel so stupid. I just fell off the boardwalk. Could you help me get out?"

Lori felt something skim across the top of her head. She crouched deeper in the water and looked anxiously about. "Hey," she called up to the dark boathouse, and this time louder. "Can you give me a hand?"

"I'm a little short on those." The gull shifted his stance on the concrete manatee statue behind her. "Couldn't even give you much of a leg up."

Lori froze. "Who said that?"

"I did."

Lori stared straight ahead. "Who's there?"

"I am."

"You, *who*?" She glanced over her shoulder at the mossy statue.

"My mother named me Maurice." The seagull began

28

preening his feathers and admiring his reflection in the water.

"Maurice," Lori snorted. "As in 'Maurice the Manatee'? That's cute."

"Don't be absurd." The gull ruffled his feathers. "Everyone knows *he* can't talk."

"Then I suppose I'm talking to..." Lori took a deep breath. "Well, then I suppose I *think* I'm talking to YOU?" She raised her eyes and stared at the gull. "I'm standing here in the freezing water, talking to a stupid *bird*?"

"We were having a perfectly civilized conversation until you started getting snippy." Maurice opened his wings to fly off.

"I HAVE BECOME MY GRANDMOTHER!" Lori pounded the water with both fists and began hobbling toward shore.

"Your grandmother?" Maurice paused mid-flap. "Who's your grandmother?"

"Not that it makes any difference, but her name is Nancy Henderson. She owns Mom's—"

"—Bait and Snack Shack," the seagull finished her sentence. He inspected the wet girl closely. "That makes you Lorelei."

Lori nodded dumbly.

"So it worked." Maurice chuckled softly.

"Yeah, I guess so." Lori looked at him. "No, wait, what do you mean, it worked?"

"Their little plan. Brilliant, brilliant, I must say."

"Well, can you say it a little faster, Maurice? My feet are killing me."

"Oh brilliant, simply brilliant!" the gull repeated happily. "The Portal has opened and the becoming is beginning!"

"The becoming is beginning. *What?*"

The bird didn't reply. His body shook as he laughed to himself.

"Listen, Maurice, I'd love to stay and chat for a while, but I gotta get out of these shoes..." Lori's voice drifted away as one Nike, then the other, floated up behind her.

"The becoming is beginning! The becoming is beginning!"

"Yeah, and you're beginning to sound more like some crazy parrot than a seagull." Lori stumbled in the soft river bottom.

"Look!" He nodded to the water. "The Portal has opened!"

"I know, I know, and the becoming is beginning."

"Indeed!" Maurice opened his beak and began panting.

Lori looked down. The water around her was glowing like someone had lit a big fire under her. But her legs weren't hot, they just felt strange like they were being compressed. "You mean I'm becoming, what? Like a fish or something?"

"Or something." The bird cocked his head and studied her with its bright black eye. "Looks to me you're becoming a manatee."

"A *sea cow*?" Lori cried as the seams of her jeans ripped apart and a bulbous gray form surged up her body.

The bird nodded.

Lori's rapidly disappearing knees buckled. "Oh this is just great," she muttered. Buttons popped off her shirt. She clutched the front as the fabric split up the back with a loud *rip*.

"An ugly old sea cow! And I was named after a beautiful river nym-" Her head disappeared under the water and a large bubble burst to the surface with an indignant "-ph!"

"Well, I think she's beautiful," the seagull sighed, admiring the smooth dark shape that melted into, then vanished beneath, the black water. He gave his wings a quick flap and returned to his perch on top of the boathouse.

Black water closed around Lori. She sank to the muddy river bottom with a bump. Terrified, she clamped her lips shut and held her breath. *Okay, this is better,* she thought as she began to rise. The world spun slowly. Lori broke the surface belly up. *Manatees are round, very round* she thought. *And buoyant, apparently. The trick is making it work for me.*

Lori's arms were now two stubby flippers with four gray fingernails attached to the end of them. The flippers bent up and down like her old hands. She waggled them. *Maybe if I move this thing like this...*

She reached out, stirred the water with her right flipper, and made a lazy circle. She added her left flipper and skimmed across the water in a smooth backstroke. *Not bad.*

Her tattered jeans were caught on the end of her paddle-shaped tail. *I can probably get around better without these,* she thought. She gave her rear end a quick flip and found herself upside down staring at an oyster bed. Twisting her body, she avoided grazing the sharp shells with her belly. *Now we're on to something!*

Lori began swimming awkwardly, experimentally, bobbing her head up and down like she had seen porpoise do. *Just wait till I tell Grandmama about this,* she thought. She paused mid-bob. *How can I ever tell her about this,* she wondered.

31

And what exactly is *this?*

That seagull said 'The Portal has opened and the becoming is beginning.' Looks like I've become a full-blown manatee, but why? And what do I do now?

Lori paddled thoughtfully. *A portal is some kind of door, isn't it? And if a door opens*—she realized with a start—*it also closes!*

Though she was covered in a warm layer of fat, Lori shivered. She tried to look at the boathouse but her head wouldn't turn—manatee necks are fused to their spines. She turned her whole body toward the boathouse and splashed back to Indian Point.

"Hey, Maurice," she called into the darkness.

"You again?" he yawned over the roof edge. "Back so soon?"

"It's not as early as you think, lazy bones. Look, the sun's coming up."

The bird squinted over his left shoulder. "Oh, so it is. How goes your adventure?"

"Maurice, I've gotta get out of here. I don't belong in the river, my grandmother's the only person I've got left, and she's at home on dry land. If I'm not there when she wakes up, I don't know what it will do to her. Please, won't you help me?"

The bird swooped back down onto his perch on the concrete manatee. He studied Lori. He liked Mrs. Henderson—the old lady was always good for a handful of breadcrumbs. On the other wing, this had to do with *them* and did he have any business interfering?

Lori's small eyes stared up at him from the water. He avoided her gaze.

"Maurice, please. You said before, when I first started changing, that you could see the Portal opening. Look into the water again. Can you see it now? Is it still open? Can I get back through it?"

"Patience, patience!" The bird held up a wing. "One thing at a time."

Maurice cocked his head and looked into the water, down past the girl, and searched the river bottom. "Mother told me about this when I was small," he muttered to himself. "Up until tonight I thought it was just a story—something you told naughty little boys and gulls to keep them from leaving the nest too soon." He pitched his voice higher and squawked, " 'Don't you fly off without me or you'll wind up falling into the Portal!' Fluff and nonsense!"

Maurice ruffled his feathers and tried to focus his thoughts as well as his eyes. He blinked, looked away, then returned his startled gaze to the mud. A large rectangle glowed softly up through the silt. "I've found it!"

"Great! Now what?"

"Well, I suggest you return to the boathouse."

Lori swam past the concrete manatee and hovered near the dock. "I don't feel anything."

Maurice peered down into the water. "You're above the Portal, but not connecting with it. Can you touch it with your tail?"

Lori tried lowering her tail, but it floated back up behind her. "How about if I turn upside down and touch it with my hands, uh, flippers?" She prepared to dive.

"No!" Maurice squawked. "If I remember correctly, whatever touches the Portal, changes first. That means your hands and arms will begin the progression while your head is still under water."

33

They pondered this in silence.

"How long can you hold your breath?"

Lori mulled it over. Once when she was little she had timed herself at about a minute. She told him.

"And then how will you get out?" Maurice added. "You were stuck down here when you were in human form."

"I can swim to shore."

Maurice shook his head. "Mother always ended her lecture with 'One way in, one way out.' You'll need to make a straight exit from the Portal just like the direct entrance you made when you fell into it. Nothing round-about allowed."

The horizon was turning pink.

"I'll worry about that after I start changing," Lori said. "Maurice, I've gotta hurry—my grandmother will be waking up any minute."

"Then begin if you must, but I don't have to watch." The gull turned around on the statue's head.

Lori looked at the sunrise glowing to the east, then at the Portal beneath her. As the one grew stronger, the other seemed to weaken.

She took a deep breath and dove.

Lori didn't have far to go—the water had only come up to her shoulders when she fell in. She planted her head in the mud and paddled frantically to keep from rising back up to the surface. Debris swirled about her face changing the water from clear black coffee to hot chocolate. Lori had no way of knowing if she was connecting with the Portal or not. All she could do was hold her breath and hope.

Her lungs began tightening. Lori let a few air bubbles escape from her nostrils. How long would she have to stay like this before the transformation took place?

Something tickled her forehead. Lori tried to brush it away, but her flippers wouldn't reach that far. Now her lungs were burning. Water got up her nose. She couldn't stay under any longer! Coughing and crying at the same time, Lori spun and flicked her tail. She broke the surface of the water and threw her arms out for balance.

Her arms? It had worked!

"Maurice! Maurice! Look!"

The startled seagull tumbled headfirst off the concrete manatee. He righted himself, shook the water off of his feathers and floated up to the girl.

"But I've still got this." Lori rolled onto her back and flipped her tail for him to see. Her teeth began chattering. "If I don't get out of this water soon, I'll get hypothermia." She stretched her arms over head. She was still four feet from touching the pier.

"Porpoise leap out of the water," she said to the seagull. "I've got a tail just like theirs—why can't I do it?"

She rolled onto her belly and flicked her tail. She landed face-first on the water. "I'm not ready for Marineland," she sputtered, "but this has *got* to work." She leaped again. This time her hands grazed the bottom of the pier.

Maurice squawked and flew to the boathouse roof.

Lori swam an awkward circle—her bony human arms and torso were no match for the heavy tail that tried to upend her. She repositioned herself and focused on the boards above. Her tail sank, dragging the rest of her body with it. "No!" she cried, struggling to remain on the surface.

The crisp morning air chilled her skin as Lori escaped the river. She clung to the edge of the boardwalk, listening breathlessly to the drip, drip of the dark water as it streamed off her skin. She was heavy, so heavy.

Her fingers began to slip.

One more time!

Lori thrashed her tail with her remaining strength. Her arms bent, her stomach scraped against the planks. She pulled herself into the boathouse and lay on the floor shivering, shaking—terrified about what was to happen next. Was she going to stay half girl, half manatee? In answer to her silent prayer, Lori's legs separated, her tail faded away. Her feet were left touching at the ankles.

Goosebumps reminded the girl that her clothes were in tatters somewhere on the river bottom. She crawled into a corner of the boathouse and looked around. There was nothing in the building to put on. She peeped out into the early morning light. Her windbreaker was in a heap at the foot of the pier.

Lori listened to the world waking up around her: Geese called to each other as they flew south in formation, a blue crab scuttled through the marsh grass. If anyone human was in the park they were too quiet to hear, and Lori was too cold to care. Hugging the wall, she slid out onto the boardwalk, grabbed her jacket, then dashed back to the safety of the shadows.

Maurice fluttered onto a rafter.

"What do I do now?" Lori asked.

The bird cried out, but Lori could no more understand him than he could her. They looked at each other, both thinking that if the girl weren't standing there dripping wet, neither of them would have believed what had just happened.

Lori squinted through a crack in the boathouse wall. Miss Glenda's laundry line was nearby, and the woman had left a pair of jeans and a couple of towels hanging out over night. Lori dashed across the park, yanked the jeans off the line, and ducked inside the carport in one smooth movement.

She was home before her grandmother awoke.

Lori couldn't get out of bed. Mrs. Henderson placed her rough hand across her granddaughter's forehead while she waited on the thermometer. She pulled it out and read it. Lori wasn't running a fever but something was clearly wrong—the girl's hazel irises were nearly swallowed up in oversized pupils, and the circles around her eyes were deep and black.

"Are you hungry?"

Lori shook her head.

"Can you go back to sleep?"

Lori closed her eyes. They shot back open.

"Do you want me to phone the doctor?" Mrs. Henderson felt Lori's wrist. Her pulse was beating rapidly.

Lori shook her head again. "I'm okay," she forced the words out. It was hard to concentrate. So hard to do anything except go over and over what had happened the night before.

Mrs. Henderson caressed Lori's cheek. Her granddaughter did not appear to be sick, only anxious—extremely so—almost, it seemed, to the point of panicking.

"What's the matter, baby?"

"I didn't sleep last night," the girl replied. It was the truth, just not the whole truth.

Mrs. Henderson nodded. The anniversary of their family's

disappearance had her hearing crazy things out on the river. Until now, Lori had seemed so strong. Maybe it had finally caught up with her. A day off from school might do her some good.

"Will you be all right if I go in to work?"

Lori looked up at her grandmother and smiled weakly. There was no point in worrying her, she just needed to think. Time to sort it all out.

Mrs. Henderson paused in the doorway. "You'll call me if you need anything?"

Lori nodded and squeezed her lids shut.

The door softly closed.

What happened last night, Lori wondered. *Something mystical, that's for sure, but what? And why to me?*

She opened her eyes and looked around the small bedroom at all the familiar objects surrounding her. This had been her mother's room before she married. After the Sweeneys disappeared and Mrs. Henderson became Lori's guardian, it had become hers. How she loved the pink striped curtains, the botanical prints on the wall, and the soft green carpeting.

Her mother's childhood books were still neatly arranged on low shelves beside the white, four-poster bed. Lori rolled onto her stomach to look at them. Mrs. Sweeney had been an avid reader, especially of mysteries and mythology. Lori ran her finger down the spine of each book and recited the titles aloud in hopes that going over the familiar would help her calm down.

"*The Odyssey, Collected Tales of Edgar Allen Poe, Native Americans— Unusual Facts and Folklore....*" Lori pulled that third book onto the bed and opened it to the table of contents. Chapter Five, "The Timucuans" looked interesting. She flipped through the pages to the chapter. Filling the left-hand page was a crude sketch of a brave sitting on a large stone, studying a pool of water.

Looks like the statue at Indian Point, Lori thought as she began reading the opening paragraph.

The girl stopped in her reading and swallowed hard. She tried to concentrate on the page in front of her but her eye was being drawn across the book, back to the drawing of the Timucuan brave. Lori fought the urge to look at the man again. Something told her that she didn't want to.

The words now swam meaninglessly on the page in front of her. It was pointless to resist. Lori took a quick glance at the brave. That split second was enough—more than enough for her to see what she had been dreading.

Though this man's upper body was the same as the statue at Indian Point, the Native American on page 46 was distinctly different. Rather than having two lean legs on which to rest his elbows while he contemplated the pond, this man's legs were joined together.

And shaped into a manatee's tail!

Lori watched her grandmother's tail lights until the tiny red pinpoints were swallowed up by the night. She climbed off the sofa and turned off the SpongeBob marathon she had been pretending to watch, then walked into the kitchen. The plastic grocery bag was where she had hidden it earlier in the day. Lori took it from behind the pantry door and double-checked its contents. Towel? Check. Flashlight? Had that, too. The cell phone was on the kitchen table. She zipped it into a plastic baggie and added it to her kit, then stared at the message pad. Should she leave her grandmother a note? And if she did, what should it say? "Dear Grandmama, if I'm not home by sunrise it's because I've turned myself into a manatee"?

Nah, that would be too weird even for Mrs. Henderson to believe.

The screen door slapped shut behind her as Lori went into the garage to get her bike. She threaded the top of the grocery bag onto the left handgrip. The extra weight made the bike tip. Lori pushed the bag closer to the front wheel, watching carefully that it wouldn't get tangled up in the spokes. She opened the side door and rolled her bike onto the driveway. After two strong pushes with her foot, she teetered off down North Beach Street. There was no need to hurry—the last thing Lori wanted to do was catch up with her grandmother as she was launching her boat, *The Whoop-de-doo*. Tonight both of them had business at Indian Point.

Three cars passed Lori on the dark road. She was grateful for their headlights. At the foot of the Granada Bridge, street lamps at the boat launch illuminated her grandmother's pickup truck parked between two others. Mrs. Henderson was already somewhere out on the Halifax blending in with the rest of the night fishermen.

Lori coasted down Miss Glenda's driveway and stopped in the shadow of the house. A light breeze rustled the plastic bag in front of her. She felt inside it for the cell phone. Yeah, it was still there.

The place was quiet: "too quiet" as they like to say in old Westerns. Lori would have felt better if she had some tree frogs to cheer her on. All she could hear tonight, though, was her heart hammering in her ears. She laid her bike on the grass and pulled off the grocery bag. A small fishing skiff buzzed across the river in front of her. Lori focused on that comforting, man-made noise, and groped her way to the path.

After a short walk, she smelled the sulfur spring. She slowed. Was the Timucuan brave still sitting on his rock? Or was he hiding behind one of those trees over there, waiting for her to pass by so he could...

The palmettos next to her moved. Lori's heart leaped. *It was him!*

No, it was only a wild cat stalking a mouse.

Lori ordered herself to take another step forward. Her hand shook as she pulled aside a palm frond to look at the spring. A high-pitched giggle escaped her lips. The Timucuan brave was right where Lori had left him the night before, and it

didn't look like he had budged since Mrs. Hayes and her girls first put him there fifty years ago. She scurried past the stone figure unchallenged.

In another minute she reached the pier. Lori's legs stiffened when she lifted them over the rusty chain strung between the first two pilings. *Maybe this isn't such a hot idea after all*, she thought, shuffling along with leaden feet. *Maybe I ought to just go on home before I get to the...*

There was the broken place in the handrail. Lori stretched out a trembling finger and tapped the splintered wood.

So it had really happened.

She gave the railing a little shake. It seemed solid. She gripped the board and leaned out through the opening.

The Portal was glowing.

Lori's dinner surged into her throat. The grocery bag slipped from her fingers and thudded onto the dock. *Why did I come back to this creepy place?* she thought, trying not to throw up. She turned to run down the boardwalk. A stirring from inside the boathouse stopped her.

"Maurice?"

There was no answer, but someone *was* moving around in the shadows. Maybe they knew something about the Portal.

Lori took a steadying breath and stepped inside the building. "Hel—" She looked up. Her mouth froze in the "O" position.

An enormous snake was coiled up in the rafters. It turned its head towards her and began lowering itself quickly to the boathouse floor.

Lori backed out of the building into the handrail. She slid along the narrow board, following it blindly toward shore. The snake she'd just seen wasn't a cottonmouth or a rattler or any other reptile Lori was familiar with. No, this one was light-colored for one thing—an albino of some sort—and slender and long, so long that even though its head was now peering out of the boathouse doorway, Lori could see loop after loop of its body still wrapped around the beams. She reached the broken place in the railing the same time the snake's head touched the boathouse floor. Lori looked over her shoulder at the Portal then back at the snake.

A loud *clunk* made her blood run cold: The snake had just dropped the rest of its body onto the pier.

Lori chewed her bottom lip while she watched the reptile weave its way towards her. Which was worse, she wondered, jumping into the river and connecting with the Portal, or staying where she was and getting snake-bit? She clambered up onto the handrail while she tried to decide.

The snake pulled itself towards her with a scraping and scratching that raised the hair on the back of her neck. The distance between them grew shorter. Lori moaned and looked again from the water to the snake.

Moonlight glimmered off of the creature's metal tail.

Metal tail?

Lori shook her head and climbed off the handrail. "This is too much!"

"This" was not a snake, it was an anchor line, a length of thick polyester cord slithering towards her, dragging a stainless steel grappling iron behind it.

The tip of the rope slid through the opening at the broken handrail. The rope stopped, as if waiting, then convulsed, like it had a severe hiccough. A large knot appeared at the end of the rope. A tug from an unseen hand pulled the knot over the edge of the pier. The rope convulsed again and another knot was tied, this time about three feet up from the first.

Another convulsion, another knot, another tug.

The first knot splashed into the water.

When all but the last four feet of the rope had disappeared over the side, a final tug wedged the anchor solidly behind a post.

A seagull swooped off the boathouse roof.

"Maurice?"

SCAW! The bird cried, flapping its wings in her face.

Lori walked over to her grocery bag. The seagull screeched, and Lori picked the bag up. Without taking her eyes off the bird, Lori reached down and pulled off her shoes. She loaded them into the bag. Next went in her shorts and her sweatshirt. She tied the bundle to the railing and climbed obediently down the rope ladder into the icy river.

"Well, it's about time," Maurice fussed from his perch on the concrete manatee's head. "I thought you'd never get in!"

"You didn't have to be so mean," Lori sputtered back. "This is all new to me. Besides, the water's freezing, and I'm not as well insulated as you are."

"Not yet, not yet," the bird agreed. "But soon!"

Lori didn't have to look down to know what was happening. She could feel her feet join, widen and flatten as if they had been run over by an underwater steamroller. "Don't you think you could have gone a little easier on me up there? You about scared me to death with that little rope trick."

"Desperate times call for drastic measures," Maurice replied as he watched the transformation.

"Huh?"

Maurice flew back onto the boathouse roof. He looked out at a small boat anchored directly opposite them. "You'll see."

Lori closed her eyes and tried to relax. It was hard not to resist as she felt herself being dragged under water. She concentrated on the changes her body was undergoing: her arms were sucked into her shoulders, her fingers melded and flattened, the skin on her face expanded and rounded. Her ears shrank into her skull. Her eyes dimmed.

She took a deep breath and sank.

Tonight's transformation was easier than the first; Lori knew what to expect and was prepared for it. She enjoyed the sensation of water rushing over her bare skin, and she didn't feel cold any more. Actually, she didn't feel anything. It was as if her entire body had been stuffed inside a huge rubber glove like the yellow ones she wore when she helped her grandmother clean out the bait coolers. She rolled onto her back, delighted to find that the skin covering her nostrils kept her from gagging. She flipped her tail and moved slowly away from the boathouse into the channel.

"Why don't you watch where you're going?" A nasal voice whined in her ear.

"Yeah, you big galoot!" another said.

Lori watched a school of mullet zigzag away.

"Now, now," a large tarpon scolded, "that's one of those new manatees. You have to swim around them."

Lori opened her mouth. "Sorry," she bubbled. But the fish were gone. She moved along cautiously. Swimming through the Halifax River was like swimming through black ink. With the full moon shining down into the water, Lori could just make out shapes. The whiskers on her face brushed against a submerged log. She turned slowly away from it.

Lori's stomach rumbled; the chicken noodle soup she had eaten for dinner had worn off. *Time for a snack,* she thought. She rubbed her snout into seagrass growing from the river bottom, then opened her mouth for a nibble. The thin ribbons tickled her nose. Lori giggled and ran her flipper across the vegetation. Her stomach rumbled again. Pooching out her upper lip, she grasped a tendril and pulled it into her mouth. Her upper and lower teeth ground up the grass. She swallowed it. *Hmmm, tastes like spinach.*

Lori hovered over the plants, munching contentedly until her lungs began to burn. She rose to the surface, poked her snout into the night air, and blinked in the starlight.

"Tell me, oh, why won't you tell me?" a voice cried to her right. Lori turned. There was the boat Maurice had been watching. Lori could make out the silhouette of a person standing up in it shaking her fist at the sky. Her fist? It was Mrs. Henderson in the *Whoop-de-doo.*

Lori swam up silently.

"All I want is an answer," the woman implored. "Just one word. Are they alive? Tell me. Are they alive? Or are they," she sank to her knees onto the hard, damp bottom of the boat, "dead?"

Lori nudged the craft with her head.

Mrs. Henderson looked about her. "What was that?

Lori blew a soft, wet greeting from her nostrils.

Mrs. Henderson clambered to the side of the boat and peered over the edge.

Lori blew her another "Hello."

"Well hey, fella." Mrs. Henderson's voice was hoarse from crying. "What are you doing out here this time of night?"

You wouldn't believe me if I told you, Lori thought.

Her grandmother eyed the manatee with interest. "I haven't seen you before, have I?" When Lori didn't swim off, Mrs. Henderson rested her cheek against the side of the boat and smiled. "You're a gentle creature, aren't you? And from the size of you, a young one. Let me see your back." To her surprise, the manatee raised the rest of its body to the surface. Mrs. Henderson examined its gray skin. "No barnacles, no scars. Where'd you come from?"

Lori gazed into her grandmother's eyes, grateful she could distract her from her grief.

"Me?" Mrs. Henderson continued as though they were having a conversation. "Oh, I'm from around here. This is where I raised my family. Just like you will one day, I reckon." She circled her hand in the water thoughtfully. "I have a fine granddaughter. Had a daughter once, and a son-in-law, too. They were good people." Mrs. Henderson's eyes glinted oddly in the moonlight. She leaned closer to the manatee's face. "Have you seen them?"

Lori shrank away from the intensity in her grandmother's voice.

"You'd tell me, wouldn't you? C'mon, little fella, HAVE YOU SEEN MY FAMILY?"

Lori's heart ached as she watched the old woman's tears fall into the water.

The low snarl of an approaching boat broke the spell. Mrs. Henderson leaped to her feet. "Slow down, you moron," she yelled at the broad white bow. "I've got a manatee here!"

The captain of the craft couldn't hear her, and he didn't see the *Whoop-de-doo* until he was nearly on top of it. He veered to avoid a collision.

The wake from the huge twin engines swamped the smaller boat. Mrs. Henderson lurched. Her feet slipped on the wet fiberglass. She reached for the console but missed her mark. With a cry she pounded her forehead against the rail. She slid, unconscious, over the side of the boat into the river.

No one saw this but Lori. She dove and positioned herself under the sinking body. "C'mon, c'mon, c'mon..." Her grandmother settled across her back. "Gotcha!"

Lori rose to the surface, but the woman's head was still under water! She rolled over to lift Mrs. Henderson's torso out of the river. *But now what?* Lori thought. *How do I get her back to shore?*

"Hey, Frank," a man spoke from the riverbank. "Do you see what I see?"

"Where?" a sleepy voice replied.

"There. Look over there. No, next to that little boat. Don'tcha see it? Looks like a two-headed sea monster!"

"Aw, you're just seeing things," the other man scoffed.

"No, look where I'm pointing. See it? Right THERE?"

"Hey, you're right. What *is* that?"

Lori thrashed her tail, praying the fishermen would get curious enough to investigate.

"I dunno, man. Let's go check it out!"

With two quick tugs on the cord, an outboard motor buzzed to life.

"Hey," the man in the bow exclaimed, "that's the *Whoop -de-doo.* Shoulda figured Nancy'd be out here tonight. But what the—?"

The boat puttered closer. Frank reached out and closed his callused hands around the woman's arms. He pulled her gently into the boat. "Jake, man, she's out cold. We've gotta get her to the hospital!"

"Yeah, ok, but don't let me hit that log. Wait a minute, that wasn't a log, that was a manatee holding her up! But where'd it go?"

Lori had already sunk out of sight and was swimming as fast as she could back to the boathouse.

50

The Portal glowed beneath her. Lori looked at the make-shift rope ladder hanging from the boardwalk. Someone (or something) had gone to a lot of trouble to make sure she was where she needed to be in order to rescue her grandmother. She dove and buried her head in the silt. At the first tingle, she rose and clung to the rope, shivering in the moonlight.

The transformation ended; Lori pulled herself up the ladder and onto the boardwalk. Her fingers trembled as she untied the grocery bag from the railing. She scurried into the boathouse to dress. Her clothes felt weightless after that thick layering of manatee skin. She stuffed her feet into her sneakers and ran out onto the board-walk, then stopped. What should she do with the rope ladder? It'd sure been useful. Lori pulled it up and poked it out of sight in the rafters. Now to find her grandmother!

She peddled through the sleeping neighborhoods as quickly as her tired legs would allow. At Memorial Hospital, she threw her bike down on the sidewalk. Her back tire was still spinning when she ran through the double doors.

"Excuse me," Lori called to the nurse at the triage counter. "Can you tell me where Nancy Henderson is? She came in a few minutes ago."

The nurse looked at her clipboard. She shook her head.

"No one by that name has been admitted this evening."

Lori swallowed hard. Surely that fall hadn't killed her grandmother! Surely they hadn't taken her to the morgue or where ever it is you take... Lori couldn't even finish the thought.

"Are you sure?" the girl persisted. "She slipped and fell in her boat a little while ago. Two fishermen said they were going to bring her here."

The nurse double-checked her records. "No one has been admitted since 11:45 p.m. Have you tried Peninsula Regional?"

Lori hadn't thought of that. Of course, the men had taken her grandmother there! She hopped back onto her bike and peddled the five long miles over the bridge to the other hospital. By the time she got there, it was close to 2:00 a.m., and Lori was near exhaustion.

"Nancy Henderson," she gasped to the receptionist. "Please tell me which room she's in."

The lady behind the counter checked her records. "When was she supposed to have come in?"

Lori's legs went weak. "About midnight."

"I don't see anyone by that name, dear. Are you sure she came to this hospital?"

"But she has to be here," Lori said tearfully. Please check again—do you have a 'Jane Doe'? Any older lady admitted with head trauma?" At the sight of the receptionist's blank expression, Lori exploded, "Let me see that!" She grabbed for the clipboard. The woman, realizing the girl's fear, turned the paper so Lori could read it.

The last two patients were men.

Lori turned and stumbled out onto the sidewalk. All she knew to do—all she was going to be able to do—was go home and wait for news. Perhaps the fishermen who rescued her grandmother would call. Surely the police would.

She dropped her bike wearily in the front yard and nudged the front door open with her knee. She walked into the kitchen to check the answering machine.

"Just what do you mean waltzing home this time of night, missy?" a familiar voice scolded.

Lori spun around. Mrs. Henderson was seated at the kitchen table pressing an icepack wrapped in a red checkered towel against her forehead. "Grandmama!" She sank to the floor at the woman's feet.

"Yes, I am your grandmother, and also the only person left on this planet to take care of you. Where have you been?"

"Oh, Grandmama," Lori repeated, looking at the ice pack. "Are you okay?"

"I'm fine," Mrs. Henderson grumbled. "Except for being sick to death from worrying about you! What were you doing outside this time of night?"

"Looking for you," Lori replied. "I've been to Memorial Hospital and Peninsula Regional And you've been here the whole time?"

"For the past two hours, watching the clock, waiting for the police to knock on the door and tell me they've pulled you dead out of some ditch!"

Lori started to giggle. Then she threw back her head and laughed.

Her grandmother looked at her sharply. "What's so funny?"

"You wouldn't believe me if I told you." Lori answered between spasms.

"Try me."

Lori was on her feet by this time examining her

grandmother's injury. "No, it's just that there I was scared to death about you, and all that time you were *here*, worrying about me."

"What do you mean you were scared to death? You knew full well I always go out on the river when the moon's like this." Mrs. Henderson glanced away uncomfortably. "And you know I'm always home before two o'clock."

Lori peeked at the wall clock. It was now ten minutes past three.

Her grandmother eyed her suspiciously. " 'You in some kind of trouble?"

Lori laughed again nervously. "Trouble?" She chewed her bottom lip for a moment. All of a sudden this had gotten difficult. Should she make something up? Some sort of excuse for being out of the house so late? Or should she tell her grandmother the truth?

Mrs. Henderson could tell what her granddaughter was thinking. "You won't never get in trouble for telling me the truth, Lorelei. It's when you start lying to me that we're gonna have problems."

Lori sat back down on the floor and leaned against her grandmother's knees. Mrs. Henderson's clothes were still damp. "You haven't changed into dry clothes!"

The old woman studied the girl. "How did you know about them being wet?"

"I saw you fall in." Lori blurted.

"What? You were there?"

The girl nodded.

"Now we're back to square one. What were you doing out so late at night all by yourself?"

Lori didn't answer.

Mrs. Henderson's voice rose. "You weren't by yourself?"

"Yes, I was alone, because you can't really count Maurice as somebody."

"Maurice?" Her grandmother ran a mental checklist of all her granddaughter's friends. This name didn't fit in. "Who's he? Some new boyfriend?" She took Lori's silence as a confession. "Well, you just wait 'til I have a word with his folks. No self-respecting young lady has any business being out so late at night with any young buck, I don't care WHO he is!"

Lori saw things were about to get out of control. "He's a bird," she explained.

"A bird?" Mrs. Henderson snorted. "Is that what they are now? In Margo's day, you called them 'foxes'. I've met my share of 'wolves,' and have called a few men 'dogs', but now they're 'birds'?"

Lori giggled. She was so tired she couldn't think straight. Her mouth took over where her brain left off. "He's a seagull, Grandmama, nothing more than that. A plain old laughing gull that hangs out at Indian Point."

Mrs. Henderson had run out of patience. "So you want me to believe that you were out 'way past your curfew at Indian Point, alone. Only you weren't alone because you were with Maurice. But I have nothing to worry about because Maurice is a SEAGULL?"

"Yes ma'am."

Mrs. Henderson bit her lip and looked away. "You've never lied to me before, baby."

"And I'm not lying now, Grandmama." Lori rose to her knees and searched the woman's bruised face. "I was there at Indian Point, right where you were, when that boat swamped you and you fell in. I was there when the fishermen came and got you out. Grandmama, *I* saved you!"

"Oh Lori, this is bad, really bad." Mrs. Henderson's breathing grew rapid. "Frank said that when they found me, a—" she paused, it sounded too spectacular. "A manatee was holding my head up out of the water." Mrs. Henderson pushed her hands against the table top and rose unsteadily to her feet. "So you were never anywhere near me. It's all lies you've been telling me. I'm going to bed."

"You asked me where Mom and Dad were," Lori whispered.

"What?"

Lori spoke to the back of her grandmother's head. "You asked me if I had seen them. You wanted to know if they are alive or dead."

Mrs. Henderson gripped the back of her chair. "How dare you say that!"

"I'm not saying this to make fun of you, I just want you to know I was there. Listen, you called that boat driver a moron. You yelled at him that there was a manatee close by."

Mrs. Henderson's knuckles grew whiter.

"That manatee was ME!"

Mrs. Henderson turned around.

Lori hurried on before her grandmother could speak. "I was in the water off Indian Point. There's a Portal you can go through. Or connect with. Or something. Whatever, it changes you Grandmama, changes whoever touches it into a manatee."

She jumped up and faced the glaring woman. "Ask me a question about tonight. Anything. You'll see, I was there. It was me who saved you!"

There was no reply.

"You looked at me. You said you'd never seen me before.

56

That I was... that I was a young one. That's what you said, isn't it?"

Mrs. Henderson's mouth dropped open.

"You asked to look at my back. Remember?"

Mrs. Henderson stared at her granddaughter.

"And I let you. You told me you had raised your family here and that one day I would too, you reckoned."

"That was *you*?" Mrs. Henderson said dreamily as her knees failed. Lori slid a chair behind the falling woman.

"That was me."

The kitchen clock ticked away the seconds as the girl and her grandmother looked at each other.

"You saved my life? You were the *manatee* that saved my life?"

Lori nodded.

Mrs. Henderson whistled softly. "Hoo boy," was all she could say.

Lori slept fitfully. Though her body was exhausted, her mind was restless and it had replayed the night's events over and over again. When she dragged herself to the kitchen it was not quite 8 a.m., but dishes in the sink showed that her grandmother had eaten hours before. Lori stuck her head in the garage. Mrs. Henderson's truck wasn't there. Lori felt sure her grandmother was already at the bait shack. *Well,* she thought, *I might as well join her. I'll go nuts if I stay here by myself thinking about it!*

The parking lot in front of Mom's Bait and Snack Shack was full. Lori coasted past row after row of the usual pickup trucks and SUV's with their empty boat trailers. Today there were also lots of sedans—fancy cars that rarely found their way down onto that fishy pavement. She parked her bike next to the TV news van idling in the fire lane, and pushed open the door to the bait shack.

Mrs. Henderson was perched on a barstool visiting with a crowd. She smiled weakly over her audience's head at Lori. On one side of her stood a grinning Jake and on the other, a bashful Frank—the fishermen who rescued her the night before.

"Do you mean to tell us, Mrs. Henderson," a television reporter spoke in deep, honeyed tones into his microphone, "that when these two gentlemen discovered you last night, you were floating face up on top of a manatee?" He poked the microphone under her nose for a reply.

"Bert." Mrs. Henderson looked uncomfortably at the wire mesh on the end of the microphone. "If it weren't for these two fine fishermen last night, I'd have been a goner."

"But we've all heard that before these men reached you, you had first been—" the reporter waved his hand around as if hoping to pull the words from the air—"rescued by a manatee. That this manatee had pulled you off the river bottom, then held your head out of the water until these men arrived." Again he placed the microphone close to her lips. "What are your thoughts on that?"

Mrs. Henderson raised her eyes and looked across the small room at Lori. "I've done nothing but think about that. It all sounds too crazy to be true. But, since I'm here in spite of this." She touched her bandaged forehead gingerly. "And these fine folks are telling me it's because of *that,* well, I guess I think my guardian angel went swimming last night."

The reporter arched an eyebrow. "As a manatee?"

"So they're telling me," Mrs. Henderson replied. The crowd chuckled appreciatively. "Now," she announced, clearly tired of the attention. "All this talking makes me thirsty. Phil!" she called to a photographer with a PRESS badge around his neck. "I'll pose for one more picture if you'll buy the house a round of sodas."

Phil grinned. "You gonna give me an exclusive, Nancy? Gonna phone me when this mysterious manatee angel reappears?"

Mrs. Henderson glanced at Lori. "Don't expect he'll be back."

"But I'll be the first to know if he does?" the photographer persisted.

Mrs. Henderson shook her head firmly. "Hope he doesn't have to. There," she said, climbing down off the stool. "I've said all I have to say. Why don't y'all spread some of your attention over to Frank and Jake?"

She pulled up the pink Formica counter top and disappeared out the rear of the building before anyone could stop her.

Lori eased out the front door and joined her grandmother on the dock. "Quite a crowd you've got in there," she said.

"Yep." Mrs. Henderson pushed her bangs wearily off her brow. "And I hope they do more than drink their free soda and go home. It'd be nice to sell some tackle."

"Have you been here long?"

"Since before sun-up."

A small motor yacht cruised slowly by the pier. When its captain recognized Mrs. Henderson, he blasted a short greeting on his horn. Mrs. Henderson waved a tired salute. This craft's wake was gentle. Its white spume nudged the pilings four or five times before dissolving back into the river.

The warm sun and the soft rise and fall of the pier made Lori feel like a baby rocking in its cradle. "You wanna talk?" she asked through a yawn.

"Not really," Mrs. Henderson replied. "But I gotta sort things out in my head. Lori, what really happened last night?"

Lori took a deep breath and tried to put events in their proper order. "It all started two days ago," she began. "Remember when you came home from being out on the water and you thought the wind was calling for me?"

Mrs. Henderson shuddered.

"It was."

As Mrs. Henderson stared at her with a mixture of awe and terror, Lori recounted hearing the voices, falling through the rotten handrail and discovering the Portal.

"When we get home, I'll show you Mom's history book. Grandmama—" Lori paused. "Do you suppose that... well, what I'm trying to say is... Do you think it's possible that what happened to me is the same thing that happened to Mom and Dad?"

Mrs. Henderson tore her eyes away from the girl and stared out over the water.

"I mean, think about it—that was their favorite place to fish. They disappeared without a trace. Do you think it's possible that they went through the Portal, too?"

Mrs. Henderson didn't reply.

"Grandmama, I heard Dad calling me!" Lori's eyes filled with tears. "It was like he knew I was at Indian Point; that he *knew* the Portal was ready. Do you think he was calling me to help them?"

Mrs. Henderson whispered, "Or join them?" She grabbed the girl's hands. "Lori, don't you ever go back to that terrible place again, d'you hear me?"

When Lori didn't answer, her grandmother pulled forcefully until she had to look her in the face. "Promise me! D'you hear? Promise me that you'll never go back there. I don't know what I'd do if I lost you too!"

Lori studied her grandmother's short white hair, her bloodied bandage, and the worry lines etched deeply into her dark tan. She loved everything about this brave, strong woman, yet she pulled her hands gently away.

"I think I have it figured out. I'm going back through the Portal. I love you, Grandmama, but I have to find my parents. I hope you'll help me when I need you."

"Baby, don't ask me that. What would I ever do without you?"

"Help me and you won't have to do without me. Help me and we can all be together like we used to be. Grandmama, help me!"

Mrs. Henderson's shoulders sagged. Lori heard a whispered, "I can't," as she walked slowly back to the bait shack.

Mrs. Henderson didn't sleep that night. Lori dozed on a pile of blankets by the bed, constantly assuring the anxious woman that she was in the house and that they were both safe. The next day the two were busy at the bait shack taking advantage of Mrs. Henderson's sudden celebrity to sell as much bait and tackle as they could. Finally, after more than twenty-four hours of wakefulness, a contented snore filled Mrs. Henderson's room. Lori hated going against her grandmother's wishes, but she knew she had to re-enter the Portal and search for her parents. She went through the kitchen door into the garage, strung her bag of provisions onto her handlebars, and rolled her bicycle silently down the driveway.

The moon no longer hung like a shiny new quarter in the sky. Instead, it looked old and tired, and slightly flattened as if struck on one side by a celestial hammer. Lori peddled carefully down North Beach Street. When she arrived at Indian Point she climbed off her bike and clicked on her flashlight. The park felt different tonight—it was quiet, and it lacked that tension of her previous visits. The leaves rustled, but wordlessly. Frogs croaked, but only to each other. There was no message in the wind, no need for Lori to hurry, yet she was anxious to get down the boardwalk and back into the water.

Lori walked down the pier. When she reached the broken place in the handrail, she tied her bag onto one side. *Better do this now before I lose my nerve,* she thought, going into the boathouse to get the anchor line. The rope felt heavier than Lori remembered. She tossed the knotted end into the river, then positioned the anchor behind a piling.

The anchor fell backwards.

Lori stood the anchor back up.

Again, it *thunked* flat upon the pier.

Lori pushed the metal tines deep into the rotting boards and gave the anchor a good kick—she was wasting valuable time! She stepped back and watched to see if it would hold. All seemed secure.

Lori turned to take off her jacket. With a determined *clunk*, the anchor fell for the third time.

A low hiss warned her. Lori ducked as the anchor line sprang out of the water. It landed with a soggy thump at her feet. Lori threw the anchor line back into the river. The rope hovered above the water, turned, then shook itself dry over her head.

Could use a little help here, Lori thought, wiping the river water out of her eyes. "Hey, Maurice," she called to the boat-house roof. " 'You up there?" No answer. She was stuck out on the end of the pier, in the middle of the night, with a temperamental rope ladder.

Lori considered her options. Sure, she could get into the water without the ladder—she had proven that already—but getting out had been so much easier with it. What was going on? The last time she was here, the thing nearly threw *her* over the side!

She peered through the broken handrail. The river beneath her looked solid—as impenetrable as a wet wool blanket. Nothing glowed off the bottom. There was no sign of the Portal. Lori's heart sank. What was she going to do now? *Maybe I've got the wrong place*, she thought. *Maybe it was closer to the boathouse?*

She walked to the end of the pier, searching for any sign of warmth in the cold water below.

Nothing.

Lori turned and searched the opposite side of the boardwalk. Nothing that way either. The Portal was gone; she had missed her chance to search for her parents. Lori pounded the handrail with both fists. She glared at the stars. "Why won't you help me?" she yelled.

A bright light from shore blinded her. Lori threw her hands up to shield her night-widened pupils.

"Don't move, and let me see your face," a man demanded.

Lori squeezed her lids shut and did as she was told.

"Miss Sweeney!" the man exclaimed once her hands down. "What are you doing here?"

It was Officer Barker.

"Miss Hayes phoned about a trespasser," he said, and Lori could tell by the tone of his voice that he felt sorry for her. That he was pitying her. That he was thinking, "Oh great, she's gone crazy just like her grandmother, and from now on I'll have *two* Sweeney women howling at the moon!"

Lori looked past the policeman to the petite figure clutching a faded blue bathrobe about her throat. "Miss Glenda!" She darted past the officer to the woman. "I've found it!"

The woman reached up a gnarled hand and pushed gray,

frayed bangs off her wrinkled forehead. Lori braced herself for a crone's "Eh, my pretty?" but instead heard a gentle, "I'm sorry, what did you say?"

"The Portal, Miss Glenda, or whatever it is they call it. I've found it! The way into the water! You know, the door you've been looking for?"

"Come along, Lori," Officer Barker said, taking the girl's elbow and steering her towards the police car. "Leave Miss Glenda alone. She's had enough excitement for one night."

Lori twisted her head over her shoulder. "Miss Glenda, you've gotta believe me!"

"Officer," the gentle voice said. "I am grateful to you for coming out this evening, but please, leave the girl with me. She's not going to cause any more trouble, and I will see that she gets home safely."

The policeman stopped. He looked from one face to the other. "You don't want to press charges?"

"Heavens no," the woman said. "Please, go on. And thank you again for your help."

Officer Barker shrugged, climbed into his patrol car, and drove off.

Lori grabbed Miss Glenda's hand. "I've found it!" She pulled the woman toward the boathouse and pointed into the river. "The way into the water. The way to my family. And yours!"

The woman looked down where the girl was pointing. "I don't see anything, dear."

"I know, that's the trouble. I found it just fine the other nights, but now it's gone. I don't know what happened to it. Maybe if we wait out here a little longer. Maybe I don't have my timing right."

"Now, why don't you come on into the house," Miss Glenda replied soothingly. "We can wait for it there."

"Didn't you hear me, Miss Glenda? I found the Portal!" Lori clutched the woman's sleeve. "You don't believe me, do you? You think I'm making this all up."

"Of course I believe you, dear, but you're nearly frozen. You need to get out of this night air before you get sick. Come with me." Miss Glenda tugged the girl's wrist. "I'll fix you a nice cup of tea. Young people still drink tea, don't they?"

"Then you'll listen to me?"

"I'll listen to every word," the woman assured Lori as they crossed the Hayes' driveway.

Lori tried to smile in spite of her trembling lower jaw. Were her teeth chattering because she was cold? Or because she was about to go into Crazy Glenda's house?

"Watch your step," Miss Glenda cautioned, opening her front door and leading Lori into the dark living room.

Lori winced as she crossed the threshold. Was she going to trip over a rug made out of some dead animal? Who knew what she'd find hanging off the walls at Crazy Glenda's house!

Miss Glenda flipped a switch; the room came into view. A surprisingly nice room—no stuffed animal heads, no elephant's foot tables. The furnishings were clean and feminine, more like Mrs. Henderson's than Ripley's Believe it or Not.

I'll put the kettle on," Miss Glenda said as they walked into the kitchen. "Won't you have a seat and make yourself comfortable?"

Lori perched herself awkwardly on the dainty fruitwood chair the woman pointed out to her. Her first inclination was to lean back and kick her shoes off, but when she saw the cheery cotton tablecloth and the starched white napkins, she realized she was in a lady's home, not a fish camp. Miss Glenda hummed a little tune as she fussed about in the cabinets for teacups and sugar. When the dainty porcelain was placed before her, Lori threaded her index and middle fingers carefully through the tiny handle. The cup teetered, and its contents sloshed, as she drew them towards her mouth.

"Wow, this is good," Lori said after draining her cup. "This tea's different. Smells spicy."

Miss Glenda pulled another chair from the corner and joined Lori at the table. It's called 'Constant Comment,'" she explained, refilling Lori's cup. "It always reminds me of my mother. It was her favorite, especially with a little squeeze of orange blossom honey."

Miss Glenda sipped her tea and traced the flowers on the tablecloth with the end of a sterling spoon while she waited for Lori's teeth to stop chattering. When the girl seemed more comfortable, she spoke.

"What do you know about me, Lori?"

Lori's cup clattered down onto its saucer. "Know about you?" she repeated in dismay.

"Yes, what do you know about me? Really know—as a fact—about me?"

"I guess I know what everybody around here knows." Lori shrugged uncomfortably. "How your family got eaten up by alligators and all."

"But now you *know* differently about that, don't you?"

Lori paused for a moment then nodded.

"What else?"

The girl stared into her cup. "I know they took you... That you went away a long time ago."

"Do you know why?"

"No ma'am." Lori squirmed in her chair. She looked at the stove to see what time it was.

"What does the town say?" Miss Glenda persisted.

"Well, people say what they want to say."

"And they believe what they want to believe, don't they, Lori?"

Lori didn't answer. She knew townspeople felt the same way about her grandmother as they did about Miss Glenda.

"They say I went crazy, don't they?"

Lori forced the slightest nod.

"That I went insane so they had to put me away before I could hurt myself. Or anyone else?"

Lori nodded again.

"That I spent my entire adult life bouncing off the walls in a rubber room?"

Lori looked desperately around the kitchen for an excuse to leave.

"Well now, don't you worry." Miss Glenda reached across the table and gave Lori's hand a brisk pat. "They only had me locked up for a little while.

"After that, I became a mermaid."

"A mermaid," Lori repeated dreamily. Her eyes rolled to the top of her head. *I'm not believing this.*

Miss Glenda rose from her chair and left the room. Lori pushed herself to her feet and walked unsteadily to the kitchen door. Miss Glenda returned as the girl began twisting the knob.

"I have something to show you."

The woman's tone said she was pleased. Pleased with her find. Or, perhaps, pleased with herself—that her trap had worked! That she had succeeded in luring one of the townspeople into her home and that now she could exact her revenge!

Paper rustled. Lori heard Miss Glenda sit down and pour out another cup of tea. The girl's curiosity got the better of her. Whatever was going on behind her back didn't sound particularly sinister. She turned around. Miss Glenda was smiling at a simple wooden picture frame. She motioned the girl closer.

Lori joined her at the table. Before them was a faded color photograph of a young woman with long red hair, smiling as she sat on a giant clamshell. The woman's hair floated about her face.

Lori stared—the picture had been taken under water!

The woman in the photograph wore a silvery bikini top

and... Lori shook her head to clear it... A fish tail?

Printed across the bottom of the photograph was "Greetings from Weeki Wachee Springs."

Lori collapsed in her chair in a fit of giggles. "Miss Glenda," she gasped, "you were a mermaid at Weeki Wachee?"

The woman nodded.

"That is too cool! My parents took me there for my ninth birthday! I loved watching you all swim. What a great job! How'd you get to do it?"

The older woman smiled at the image before them. "The hospital released me after two weeks of intensive grief counseling. My therapist suggested that I move someplace new, someplace where my memories wouldn't be so painful. Since I was an excellent swimmer, (Mama saw to that since she kept losing her family to the water!) the springs hired me on as a mermaid. Those were six wonderful years."

"What was it like? Was it hard holding your breath for so long?"

"The coaches start new mermaids out slowly, dear, so they can build up their lungs. And, of course, there are underwater air hoses to breathe from. At my strongest, though, I could hold my breath for over two minutes."

"What did you do after you quit working there? You didn't come back to Ormond."

"No, I stayed at the park and managed the gift shop. Until last summer, that is, when I retired."

"A mermaid at Weeki Wachee," Lori repeated happily to herself. "You weren't afraid to go back into the water, after all, y'know, that happened to your family?"

"Honey, that only happened here, and then only once in a blue moon."

"Once in a what?" Lori frowned.

"Blue moon," Miss Glenda repeated. "You've heard that old saying, haven't you? Such and such happens only 'once in a blue moon'?"

"Yes ma'am," Lori's voice trailed off. Her eyes swept over the kitchen walls. "Do you have a calendar?"

Miss Glenda pointed to the right. "There's one hanging inside that cupboard."

Lori hopped up and pulled the cabinet door open.

"What is it, dear? Have you forgotten something?"

"No ma'am." Lori squinted at the calendar. She ran her finger down the column of Fridays. "I just remembered something. Aha!" She jabbed the last Friday of the month with her index finger. "Here it is."

"Here *what* is?"

Lori pulled the calendar off its peg and brought it over to the kitchen table. "Miss Glenda," she said, smoothing the paper flat with her palm, "do you know the dates your family disappeared?"

The older woman thought. "1957, 1964..."

"No ma'am, I mean the actual days." Lori bit her lip as she flipped through the rest of the calendar.

"I could get you as close as the months, Lori. Why?"

The girl didn't immediately answer. Instead, she spun the calendar so the woman could read it. "Do you notice anything unusual about last Friday?"

"October thirtieth, no national holiday or anything." Miss Glenda furrowed her brow as she looked up at the girl.

"What else do you see in that square?" Lori persisted. "What kind of a moon do they have printed there?"

"A full moon, dear. Remember how bright it was?"

73

Lori drew her finger up the page to October first. "A full moon like this?"

"I suppose one is pretty much like any other. Lori, what is this all about?"

"Miss Glenda, my parents disappeared the night of a full moon. And I've heard the stories—every member of your family disappeared during a full moon, too. Am I right?"

Miss Glenda nodded.

"Now do you, by chance, know the meaning of the phrase 'Once in a Blue Moon' ?"

Miss Glenda rubbed her temples. "Dear, you're speaking in riddles. What does this have to do with anything?"

"It explains *everything*," Lori replied softly. "Miss Glenda, I don't suppose you're on-line, are you?"

"I've got, what do you call it?—broadband. But what does that have to do with—?"

"Humor me, please. Where's your computer?"

"In the next room. I'll show you." Miss Glenda led the girl into a small sunroom. Lori sat down at the keyboard.

"I'm bringing up the calendar for the year my parents disappeared," Lori explained as she tapped on the keys. She expanded the view for October, three years ago. At October second she paused, then she scrolled through the month. At October thirtieth, Lori stopped. And stared. And began to cry.

"Lori, if you don't tell me what this is all about, I *am* going to go crazy."

Lori pointed to the first date and then to the second. "What do you see?" she asked.

"I see a full moon and another full moon."

"Miss Glenda, the phrase 'Once in a Blue Moon' describes

an event that happens rarely. Just every so often. The phrase came about because sometimes a month will have two full moons in it. Early calendar makers would color in that second, and very special, full moon with blue ink to make it stand out." She smiled at the astonished woman. "Don't ask me how I know this—probably learned it watching 'Jeopardy' with my grandmother.

"Anyway, I had my experience with the Portal last Friday. During a Blue Moon. My parents vanished three years ago on Saturday, October 30th, another Blue Moon. I am willing to bet everything I own that each and every member of your family disappeared during a Blue Moon, too."

Miss Glenda sat heavily in her chair. "Look these up," she whispered. "August, 1957; September, 1964; March, 1969."

Lori's fingers flew over the keys. Each time she accessed a date, she nodded.

"My word." The shaken woman turned her eyes to the girl. "What do we do now?"

"Find out when the next one is," Lori replied, and kept typing.

"Grandmama, we're in luck," Lori concluded after telling Mrs. Henderson about the previous night. "There's another Blue Moon next year, beginning January the 29th. Isn't that great?"

Sunlight streaming through the kitchen window accentuated the lines criss-crossing Mrs. Henderson's face, but the dark circles under her eyes were gone. She had enjoyed a good night's sleep. She was refreshed, and she was furious.

"Am I going to have to change the locks on the doors to keep you home?" Mrs. Henderson scowled at Lori. "Do I have to send you off to some boarding school to keep you away from that cursed place?"

Lori was confused. She had expected her grandmother to be happy about last night's discovery. The way Lori saw it, if her parents had become manatees, they wouldn't have wanted to roam too far from the Portal. Once winter came and the Halifax River cooled, however, the Sweeneys would have had to migrate to warmer waters along with all the other manatees. And where was the closest spring? Blue Spring, in Orange City, was only forty minutes away, and Lori was going there on a field trip in two days.

"I thought you'd want Mom and Dad home more than anything in this world," Lori said, her eyes welling up with tears.

"I've told you, Lori, I've already lost them. The thought of losing you, too... well, I can't go there." Mrs. Henderson rose slowly from the kitchen table. Her knees buckled as she stood. Lori leaped to her feet to help. Mrs. Henderson shook her head and pushed her granddaughter away. She leaned against the table, then wiped her forehead with the back of her hand. Without saying another word, Mrs. Henderson shuffled out of the room.

****

Lori dreamed she was at Indian Point. She was looking at the Hayes' boathouse, but instead of it being the one-room shack she knew, the building had been transformed into a tower. She craned her neck to see the top of it.

The column was tall—so tall that the empty rooms, stacked haphazardly one on top of the other, swayed in the night breeze as they strained to touch the full moon glowing blue above them. Bare light bulbs burned in the ceiling of each room, and tattered sails hung in each of the broken windows. A gust of wind sent the wisps of fabric fluttering like ghostly fingers beckoning Lori to come closer, closer.

A boat roared by. The tower rose and fell as the wake crashed into the pier. When water splashed against her face, Lori realized that it wasn't the pier that was rocking, but her. She was in the Halifax River!

She swam towards the boathouse and, as she neared it, the light in its uppermost room went out. Lori swam faster. The second room went dark, then the one below it. Lori pushed harder against the current, but the faster she moved, the faster the lights blinked out down the column. By the time she reached the pier, a single bulb was left burning. Lori grabbed the nearest piling, desperate to reach that one light.

The moon disappeared. The world went black. Lori looked up. An enormous bat flitted back and forth over her head. The creature swooped. Lori ducked under water to avoid its sharp claws. When she could hold her breath no longer, she rose cautiously to the surface.

The bat was gone.

The pier was empty.

As pieces of the shattered boathouse floated past her, Lori awoke—her heart heavy with despair she didn't understand.

The bus ride to Blue Spring began at 8:30 a.m. Lori was grateful for the early start—most of her classmates weren't yet fully awake, and the quiet gave her a chance to go over her plans. The bus rumbled across the parking lot and stopped under a large oak heavy with Spanish moss. "Watch your step," the driver cautioned each of his passengers as they pushed each other up the aisle. "Be back here by two o'clock sharp, or be prepared to walk home," he called after each student's back. Once the bus was empty, the man reclined his seat and shook open the morning's News-Journal.

Lori was one of the first to disembark. She had sat up front by the teacher and chaperones to avoid Bobbie and Brenda. She stepped off onto the warm asphalt and walked toward the picnic pavilion. Ranger Wayne Hartley was already there pointing out the girls' bathroom to the right and the boys' to the left. Lori sat as close to the man as she could—she didn't want to miss a word.

"I want to wish you all a good morning," the ranger began pleasantly once his audience was settled on the wooden benches. "Your teacher picked a great day for you to be here—that cold snap brought us a lot of manatees. We'll start out by the river and then we'll follow the nature trail through the woods over to the boil. Have any of you been here before?"

Three hands went up.

"Fine, this'll be a great surprise for the rest of you. Please do not disturb any of the plant life, and stay on the boardwalk at all times. Anyone leaving the designated trail will spend the rest of the day on the bus. Am I understood?" The class nodded. "Then let's go meet our guests."

Lori stayed close to the ranger as they walked down the slope to the path that paralleled the St. John's River. When she reached the water's edge, she was startled by the logjam in front of her. *How are the manatees supposed to swim through that?* she wondered. On closer inspection, she realized that the river wasn't clogged with tree trunks: the long, brownish objects floating on top of each other in the clear, spring water *were* the manatees. Lori grinned as a calf rose from the sandy bottom to nurse from behind its mother's flipper. She laughed with joy at the sheer number of animals co-existing without any hint of aggression.

Mr. Hartley stopped in front of a glass-front display case. The class formed a semi-circle. "Here are drawings of our regulars," he said, pointing to simple outlines of twelve different manatees. "A lot of people say they can't tell the animals apart—that they all look the same. Well, if it weren't for boats, that would be the case. But, as you can see here, propeller wounds leave distinct scars. Take Crazy Nick, for example." The man pointed to the first figure. "You can tell him apart from Beauty by this." He ran his finger down the crescent shaped line drawn on the animal's back. "All their injuries are different, and just when you think you've got everyone identified, somebody gets a fresh wound and you have to change the board."

Lori looked past the man's shoulder to the spring. If she was going to identify her parents she'd need more information. "How can you tell how old they are?"

"Get your grandmother to ask them!" Bobbie hissed from the back row.

Lori's ears turned red. The muscles between her shoulder blades tightened.

"We're still learning a lot about manatees," Mr. Hartley admitted, "but we can get a rough idea of their age from their size. Newborn calves are about three feet long and weigh about sixty pounds. They grow quickly—an orphaned calf raised at SeaWorld weighed nearly four hundred pounds by the time she was two years old. Most full-grown manatees average ten feet in length and weigh around fifteen hundred pounds."

Lori raised her hand timidly. She hated to draw attention to herself, but she was afraid that if she didn't ask the right questions, she wouldn't learn what she needed for her plan to succeed. "How do they get here to the spring?"

"Through the St. Johns River," Mr. Hartley said. "How they get into the St. Johns, that's a story in itself. Our trackers have plotted just about every migratory route imaginable."

"Your trackers?" Lori's teacher asked.

"Yes, organizations like the Sirenia Project have volunteers who tag the manatees, track them, and then pass the information they've gathered along to us."

"Does it hurt to tag them?" a boy asked.

"Not at all," Ranger Hartley replied, leading the class toward the observation platform. "We don't attach anything permanently to them like what you see on cattle—you know, like a brand or a piece of plastic that's clamped to their ear. Instead, we fasten a narrow belt around the base of the manatee's tail. Attached to that belt is a four-foot long flexible nylon tether and a floating tube with a satellite transmitter inside it. The transmitter emits radio signals to a polar orbiting satellite giving the manatee's location, its activity, and the water temperature. Researchers can access this information daily on their computers. The tag assembly doesn't hurt the manatee or restrict its freedom of movement, and it's designed with a 'weak link' so it'll break loose if it gets tangled in vegetation or debris."

The group stepped up the concrete steps onto the observation deck.

"Well, now, here comes Li'l Gal." Ranger Hartley pointed to a manatee that had separated from the herd. "We tagged her and a young male that we named Buster this summer. They seem to prefer cruising up and down the Halifax River."

The manatee swam through the clear water toward the observation platform; the transmitting device attached to her tail looked like a floating soda can with a long straw sticking out of it.

"Like clockwork." The man chuckled when the animal poked her bristled snout into the air. "She's been wintering at the spring for the past three years. Every time we have a group of school kids out here on the platform, she and Buster swim over to take a look. I don't see him right now. Sure hope nothing's happened to him.

"Huh," the ranger said quietly, "it looks like she's lost a lot of weight. Hello Li'l gal," he called tenderly. "You doing all right?"

The manatee swam up to the observation deck, and the de-

lighted children jostled each other for a better position across the guardrail. Li'l Gal paddled slowly along the edge of the platform seeming to study each child's face as she passed.

Lori's knees went weak. "You say she's about three years old?"

"Well, nobody knows for sure, but she and Buster first showed up, let's see... Yep, it was three years ago this month. We remember the first time we saw them because they were just little things. Must have gotten separated from their mothers."

As the manatee glanced at each child, Lori pushed her way to the guardrail and fell to her knees. She poked her head under the barricade and lowered her face as close to the water as she could.

"Here, here," one of the parents scolded.

Ranger Hartley moved to pull Lori to her feet. Just then Li'l Gal paddled over. She hovered inches below the girl's face. The two regarded each other silently.

Lori smiled.

The animal looked intently at Lori, then blew a wet greeting.

Ranger Hartley leaned over the railing next to Lori. "I've never seen her do that before," he said, pushing his hat off his forehead and scratching his head.

"Hey Lori, maybe that's the one that 'saved' your grandma," Bobbie jeered. But nobody laughed; the class was fascinated.

Lori wasn't aware of anything but the soft "whoof" from the manatee floating below her.

Bobbie picked up a rock. "Watch me make that ugly thing go away," she whispered to Brenda. The girl pulled her arm back and launched the stone.

Li'l gal squealed and dove.

"Bobbie!" Lori leaped to her feet. "You are *such* a jerk!"

The blonde spun to face the class. "It gave me the creeps!" She sneered at Lori. "You both do!"

Ranger Hartley grabbed Bobbie's shoulder. "For your information, it's both a state *and* federal offense to harm, injure, kill or disturb a manatee." He glared at the girl, the muscles in his jaw working angrily. Finally he said, "Let's walk up to the boil."

Lori dusted off her knees. She would wait for her class on the bus. She smiled: she'd seen what she had come to see.

"So here's the plan," Lori said, resting her elbows on the flowered tablecloth. She shook her head when Miss Glenda raised the teapot. "Not for me, thanks, but you're probably gonna need some." She grinned when the older lady shuddered. "It's not that bad, really.

"January 29th is the first night of the Blue Moon. As soon as the Portal starts glowing, I'll transform and start swimming towards Blue Spring.

"See what you think," Lori said, unfolding an area map. "If I go south to Edgewater, then cut across Mosquito Lagoon, I can enter the St. Johns River. The St. Johns takes me into the spring. I'll meet up with Mom and Dad, and bring them back here the same way."

Miss Glenda furrowed her brow as she considered the map before them. "But Lori," she said after a long pause. "It won't work."

Lori jabbed the blue lines. "Of course it will. See, the Intercoastal Waterway connects with the St. Johns here, then it's a straight shot into Blue Spring."

Miss Glenda ran her finger across the map. "It's too far." She shook her head. "There's no way you'd have time to swim all that way down and back."

"Then I'll go north," the girl announced.

"That's too far, too, Lori. The Intercoastal Waterway doesn't connect with the St. Johns until you get to Jacksonville. There just isn't enough time." Miss Glenda looked at the girl sadly. "You would be caught waiting for the next Blue Moon, and that isn't for another two years."

"Mom and Dad did it!"

"They had more than three days."

Lori absorbed the bad news in silence. The truth of Miss Glenda's words sank in.

"It won't work," Miss Glenda repeated.

Lori began to cry.

Miss Glenda moved the tea things around as she thought. "Unless..."

"Unless what?" Lori looked up through wet lashes.

"Unless I drive you there."

"That won't do me a whole lot of good if the Portal is over here," Lori said.

"Drive you there *after* you've changed."

Lori sat up. "You mean while I'm, like, a manatee?"

Miss Glenda nodded.

"That could work," Lori said, rising from her chair and walking about the kitchen while she thought out loud. "When I transform it's as a calf, not as an adult. I'll weigh what—seventy, eighty pounds? Under a hundred, anyway."

"Too heavy for me to lift," Miss Glenda observed.

"Yeah, but we can hook me up to something. Hey!" Lori snapped her fingers. "There's a winch in your boathouse for raising and lowering boats."

"But what will we lower you in *to*?" Miss Glenda asked. "I don't have a boat anymore."

"No, you don't," Lori agreed. "But my grandmother does."

"Didn't you say she didn't want you transforming again?"

"Yeah, but after she hears our plan, I know she'll agree to help."

"Okay," Miss Glenda said, "so we drive one baby manatee to Blue Spring. How are we going to get that one baby manatee plus two, thousand pound adults, back over to the Portal?"

"We'll have to swim back."

"If you conserve your energy, you might survive the cold water—remember, hypothermia is a leading cause of manatee deaths—but you're talking about making a long trip in a short amount of time. Manatees are built for comfort, not for speed. They average two, maybe six miles per hour."

"On the plus side," Lori said, "we'll be in the St. Johns River, one of the few in the USA that flows north. Not having to swim against the current will help us some." She looked at the key at the bottom of her map and took out a piece of paper.

"Every inch equals fifteen miles." Lori laid the paper on top of the map. "Now I know this won't be exactly accurate, but look—one inch gets us to Lake George, another puts us close to Ravine Gardens. Three, four, five inches and we're in Jacksonville. Multiply that five by fifteen miles per inch." Lori's pencil flew over the paper. "Seventy five miles. Divide that distance by, say, six miles per hour, and in around twelve hours we're half-way home."

"Yes," Miss Glenda agreed quietly, "but that still leaves you the second part of the journey. Then you will be tired and cold *and* fighting the current."

Lori put her paper against the map again. "Five more inches puts us back in Ormond Beach."

"Twelve more hours of solid swimming," Miss Glenda said.

"We'll have three days to make the trip." Lori's voice rose as she realized how hazardous a journey she was intending to make.

"Every minute will count." Miss Glenda looked at Lori somberly.

"Every minute will count," the girl agreed.

Mrs. Henderson leaned over the railing at the municipal pier thinking about what Lori had told her and watching the river change colors as the sun set. On the shore, a blue heron stood motionless. Both their attentions were riveted on the water. A swirl near Mrs. Henderson's feet made her smile. A large manatee rose to the surface. It stared at the hose coiled at the edge of the pier.

"Sorry pal." Mrs. Henderson shook her head. "I'm not supposed to give you fresh water. You're a wild animal. You need to stay away from people and find what you need on your own. It's safer for you that way."

The creature grazed on the marsh grass, then turned south to follow the coastline. Mrs. Henderson watched his outline melt into the water and disappear.

The whine of a Jetski broke the quiet as it whizzed past the end of the pier. Its driver turned the vehicle sharply to jump its own wake. The craft caught air, then landed roughly back down on the water. The driver turned to make another pass. Sunlight glimmered off a gold medallion. Mrs. Henderson grunted. It was Joe Simpson.

Mr. Simpson revved the engine and aimed for the shallows, not far from where manatee had been grazing.

"Fool!" Mrs. Henderson muttered. "He knows he's supposed

to stay away from marsh grass!" She waved to get the man's attention, but he ignored her. Mrs. Henderson climbed over the railing into the *Whoop-de-doo*. She pulled the starting rope and motored carefully into the channel.

Mr. Simpson slowed alongside her with a scowl. "You're in my way, Nancy."

"I'm out protecting manatees," she replied curtly, "from idiots like you."

"Hey." The man looked her faded boat up and down. "I've got more money in this baby than you do in that rusty bucket, and I paid close to thirty grand for *The Love Machine*. You telling me some stupid manatee is worth more?"

"I'm telling you I don't care what your boats cost—only how fast they're going in these protected waters. It doesn't matter to the manatees whether you've got $200 or $200,000 worth of engine under you. If you hit one going fast enough, it's dead."

"Boo hoo, why don't you find a nice big tree to hug?"

"Why don't you obey the law?"

"What proof do you have that I wasn't?" He sneered. "You got me on video? No? All right, lemme guess—you've got a radar gun on board that thing, huh? You clocked me speeding and now you're gonna make a citizen's arrest."

Mrs. Henderson remained silent, loathing the man from the top of his wavy black hair to his manicured toes, and all the gold chain and gray chest hair in between.

"Well, if you don't have any proof, you can't stop me." He revved the engine, soaking Mrs. Henderson.

The woman put The *Whoop-de-doo* in reverse and backed

away.

"I didn't think so." Mr. Simpson smirked.

The flash of his too-white teeth against his too-brown skin made Mrs. Henderson feel like she was staring into the face of an oversized, smug barracuda. She twisted the throttle. The *Whoop-de-doo* leaped forward, ramming the Jetski. The smaller craft dipped under the larger boat's weight. Joe Simpson jumped off into the river, his toupee floating away on the current like a drowned river rat.

Mrs. Henderson pulled on the tiller and headed back to the pier. *That's what you get for thinking.*

Lori pressed her ear against her grandmother's bedroom door. Mrs. Henderson's slow, regular breathing assured the girl that her departure would go unnoticed. She slipped her note through the crack, then left.

It was hard for Lori to believe that it was finally time to go. At first January 29th was so far down on the calendar, so far off in the distant future, that it felt like it would never arrive—like Christmas always did when she was a kid. Then, like Christmas, it came. And, just like Christmas, the day promised to be full of surprises. *Let's hope they're pleasant ones*, Lori thought, pushing her bicycle down the driveway.

The keys to the *Whoop-de-doo* jingled in her jacket pocket as Lori peddled to the marina. The parking lot was empty, tonight's fishermen already out on the river. Lori hid her bike behind the bait shack and climbed into her grandmother's boat. She pulled the starting rope. The engine chugged to life.

Lori scanned the parking lot one last time for her grandmother, but Mrs. Henderson was safe at home where her granddaughter had left her. Lori backed out of the boat slip and turned south. With its running lights off, the *Whoop-de-doo* puttered invisibly all the way to the boathouse at Indian Point.

"Ahoy there," Miss Glenda called as Lori looped the mooring line around a cleat.

"Yo-ho-ho!" Lori replied, pulling herself up onto the boardwalk.

"Did you eat a big dinner?"

"And a peanut butter and jelly sandwich a few minutes ago." Lori rubbed her swollen stomach. "I'm stuffed."

"I'm sure you'll burn that off pretty quickly." Miss Glenda adjusted the rigging on the boat winch. She looked at her watch. "Almost time, isn't it?"

Lori nodded. "And about forty-eight hours from now you'll be back here ready to throw the rope down when we need it. Then voila—we're done."

"But how will I know what time to be out here?"

Lori chewed her bottom lip in thought. "I'll send Maurice ahead. He'll tap on your kitchen window and let you know."

"Ah, like that old poem by Edgar Allen Poe." Miss Glenda closed her eyes and dropped her voice low.

'Once upon a midnight dreary,
While I pondered, weak and weary,
Over many a quaint and curious volume of forgotten lore...' "

Lori groaned, "Please, Miss Glenda, anything but *that*!"

With a little smile and shake of her head, the woman continued:

'While I nodded, nearly napping,
Suddenly, there came a rapping,"

Miss Glenda cupped her hand to her ear.

'As of someone gently tapping!
Tapping at my kitchen door!' "

Lori rolled her eyes. "You mean *'chamber'* door."

'Quoth the seagull,'

"Seagull?" Lori objected. "It wasn't a seagull!"

" 'Never—' "

"—mind!" Lori sighed deeply.

"Or something like that." Miss Glenda curtsied to her unappreciative audience. "Oh Lori, do you think this will work?"

Lori was busy stuffing an armload of towels and clothes into a dark corner of the boathouse. "Why wouldn't it?"

"Well, have you stopped to think about how complicated this is?"

Lori brought the anchor line out. "I'm afraid if I do, I won't be able to go through with it." She tossed the rope into the river. "If I don't come out the way I go in, the transformation ought to hold, don't you think?"

Miss Glenda nodded.

The two looked at each other through the shadows.

Lori turned and fussed with the pile she had just set down. "These'll come in handy when we come out. I even found a pair of Dad's old jeans." She held up a faded pair of Levis. "Hope he can still fit into them after weighing a thousand pounds." Lori giggled. Then laughed. Suddenly she couldn't stop laughing.

Miss Glenda eyed the girl closely. "Are you sure you want to go through with this?"

"I don't have a choice." Lori took a steadying breath and pressed the jeans into her friend's hands. "We'll be back for these," she whispered.

From where they stood, the two could see the Portal opening. At first the sliver of light looked like a moonbeam reflecting off the river bottom. As they watched, the beam widened until the water under the boathouse glowed.

Lori scaled down the ladder. She peeled off her clothes, tied them to the end of the rope, and jerked her thumb upward. Miss Glenda pulled the clothes into the boathouse. The transformation began.

Headlights flashed through the treetops. A truck skidded to a stop in the parking lot. The driver's side door thumped shut. Hurried footsteps crunched across the shell path.

"The police!" Lori called up to Miss Glenda. "Turn off your flashlight!"

Miss Glenda did as she was told, but she could see that it wasn't a policeman running up the boardwalk towards them. She would have preferred a whole precinct with their guns drawn to this one person.

"We're sunk," she sighed.

It was Nancy Henderson.

"Lori!" Mrs. Henderson closed the distance between them with a sudden burst of speed. "Don't you do it!"

"It's too late, Grandmama," the girl replied, leaning back and flipping her tail out of the water.

Mrs. Henderson sagged against the railing.

Lori swam under the dock and into the sling. "Start cranking me up, Miss Glenda."

"Lorelei Marie Sweeney, you're coming out of that river before this goes any further!" Mrs. Henderson pushed past Miss Glenda to the crank handle. The rusted winch creaked and protested as its payload was raised. "Running off with my boat on some cockamamie fishing trip that I'm sure this woman talked you in to. Wait till I get you home! Many a Blue Moon is gonna rise and set before you get to leave the house after dark. Or before dark, for that matter." She made three more revolutions with the handle. "Now give me your hand young lady, I've had more than enough of this foolish—"

A juvenile manatee looked up at the women.

Mrs. Henderson's mouth dropped open. Her grip relaxed. The crank handle began to spin, lowering Lori back into the river.

Miss Glenda reached over and flipped the lock into position. "I'll go get the boat," she said quietly.

The *Whoop-de-doo* chugged to life. Miss Glenda put the boat in reverse and backed hard into the pier. The boardwalk shuddered; Mrs. Henderson rallied. "What in thunder are you doing?" she yelled over the handrail at Miss Glenda.

"It's been a little while since I've driven one of these," Miss Glenda called up apologetically. *Like about thirty years*, she thought. "I'm sure it will all come back to me in a minute."

"Time's a wastin'," Mrs. Henderson fumed, squinting down at the boat beating against a piling. "I'll drive!" She threw both legs over the railing and dropped into the boat. "Now what's this fool plan?"

****

"Tuck those blankets around her," Mrs. Henderson ordered after Lori had been lowered into the bottom of the boat. "And meet me at the ramp with my truck." She handed Miss Glenda her key ring, and waited for the woman to climb over the side into the shallows. Miss Glenda slogged through the muck toward shore. Mrs. Henderson pushed the tiller and sped to the community boat launch.

"Coming home so soon, Nancy?" Officer Barker greeted the woman as she idled the *Whoop-de-doo* next to the pier.

Mrs. Henderson glanced over her shoulder at the blanket in the bottom of her boat. She looked up at the policeman and forced herself to smile. "Yeah, I thought I'd make it easy on you tonight."

Officer Barker watched Mrs. Henderson's truck speed across the parking lot. He raised his eyebrows questioningly. Mrs. Henderson clenched her jaw and stared straight ahead. Miss Glenda threw the vehicle in reverse. The boat trailer zigzagged down the narrow concrete ramp. "That's far enough!" Mrs. Henderson barked when her truck's back tires touched the water. "Well, here's my ride, Officer." She revved the motor, cutting off further conversation. Expertly she threaded the boat onto the crooked trailer.

Officer Barker walked up to the truck and pulled open the passenger door. " 'Evening, Glenda," he called across the empty seat. Miss Glenda tapped the steering wheel nervously and studied the night sky through the wind-shield. "I didn't know you and Nancy were friends."

"Why yes, Officer, we're friends. Great friends. Life and death—I mean, lifelong friends, aren't we Mrs.—, um, Nancy dear?"

Mrs. Henderson climbed into the passenger seat. "Have a good evening, Officer," she said gruffly, tugging the door free from the man's hands and shutting it firmly in his face. "Drive, Glenda."

The truck tires spun on the wet pavement. Officer Barker leaped back to protect his toes as the trailer bounced up the ramp.

The forty minute drive to Blue Spring seemed to last an eternity. The night air was warm, and Lori was comfortable in the bottom of the *Whoop-de-doo*, but the minutes passed like hours as she bumped along Interstate 4.

Blue Spring Landing was the closest boat launch to the lagoon where Lori had seen her mother. Miss Glenda signaled and turned right into the parking lot. It was crowded with fishermen. She spun the wheel and clattered away from the ramp without slowing down.

A second boat ramp was off West French Avenue. Miss Glenda drove down Main Park Drive to the turnoff. After a sharp left they arrived at the boat launch. There were fewer trucks here, and no one loitering in the parking lot. Miss Glenda put the truck in reverse and aimed for the ramp.

Mrs. Henderson glanced at her watch—they had wasted precious time finding this second landing, and it was going to take Lori longer to reach the lagoon from up here. In another four hours it would be daybreak. "Once I've got the boat off the trailer, pull up into that spot there," she said, hopping out of the truck. "And for Pete's sake, Glenda, hurry!"

Miss Glenda parked the truck and trotted down the short pier. "You drive," Mrs. Henderson said, moving to the bow of the boat. "I want to keep an eye on Lori."

Miss Glenda started the motor. "Is she all right?"

Mrs. Henderson pulled back the blanket to stroke the top of Lori's wrinkled head. "Seems to be." Lori blew a soft puff of air. "Okay here, let's go!"

The *Whoop-de-doo* idled past a pair of nodding fishermen anchored near the eastern shore. The occupants of the boats exchanged friendly waves as is the custom. Once the women were clear of the other craft, Miss Glenda twisted the throttle.

Mrs. Henderson watched her companion dip a silver ice bucket in the river and pour it over the manatee. "Glenda, what are you doing?"

"Making Lori more comfortable. I think she got all dried out on the ride over."

Mrs. Henderson smiled faintly. "She's not a fish you know." She became serious and pointed to an outcropping of trees to the west. "Aim for that overhang. We should be hidden there."

Miss Glenda cut the engine next to a stand of Cypress trees then looped the mooring line around one of the knobby knees protruding from the water. Lori knew what to do next and turned around.

Mrs. Henderson angled a five-foot piece of plywood down the left side of the boat into the bottom. Lori crawled on her belly as far up the board as she could. "Here we go," Miss Glenda whispered. Mrs. Henderson leaned over and grabbed the edge of the plank closest to her feet. Miss Glenda grabbed her side. "One, two," they whispered together, "three!"

The board tipped; Lori slid down into the water with a soft splash. When she rose, Miss Glenda was pointing to the south.

Lori dove.

They had run out of time for good-byes.

"Stop right there!" a man demanded. "Put your hands up where I can see them!" A searchlight swept across the *Whoop-de-doo*.

Lori had seen the Marine Patrol approach. She watched now in dismay as one of the officers boarded her grandmother's boat. The man frowned at the two elderly ladies squinting in the bright light. He pointed to the plank. Lori saw the women look at each other then shrug.

"You're trying to tell us that we didn't just see you dump something overboard?" the officer asked.

"It was trash," Miss Glenda stammered.

The officer reached into his shirt pocket for a pen. He gestured with it to the water. "And you know what kind of fine you'll pay for littering?"

Mrs. Henderson glared at Miss Glenda. "It wasn't trash. It was a log we found floating out in the lake. We didn't want anyone hitting it."

"How 'bout it Stan, you see a log out there?"

The officer in the patrol boat flashed his light across the top of the water. "Nope. Current's running pretty strong, though."

"Gentlemen, I'll tell you the truth," Miss Glenda said as the officer read their drivers license information into his radio. "We were returning a young manatee that we had rescued to the wild."

"Well, that little good deed of yours could land you in jail," the man scolded. "The Florida Manatee Sanctuary Act prohibits any molesting of wildlife—that means touching them or doing what you might think is 'helpful.'" He called to the patrol boat. "See any manatees?"

Stan shook his head.

The first officer's radio chattered. He spoke tersely into the receiver then called over to the patrol boat. "Headquarters says to 'cuff 'em and bring 'em in."

"But they're just little old ladies," Stan objected. "And we've no proof that they actually had a manatee."

"They're wanted for questioning," the first officer explained, snapping a handcuff around Mrs. Henderson's right wrist and reaching for her left.

"About a manatee?" Stan asked.

"Nope, about a murder."

26

The sun broke the horizon in a brilliant orange ball. Lori let it warm her back as she double-checked her route. Without Miss Glenda to guide her she was afraid she'd miss her turn. *Okay,* she thought, *there's that bend in the river.* She dove and concentrated on making as much headway as she could between breaths. Sunlight dappled the river bottom. Lori grabbed a bite of ribbon grass as she swam over a thick patch. She was hungry. Ever since she transformed, she had been hungry. A cormorant paddled past, its sweet, high-pitched voice trailing behind it like a swirl in the water:

> "All things Bright and Beautiful,
> All Creatures, Great and Small..."

Lori recognized the hymn from church. "All things Wise and Wonderful," she hummed along. "The Lord God made them All."

She rose for a breath near an oak tree that had toppled off the riverbank. Roots hanging off its base looked like hundreds of long, skinny fingers straining to dig themselves back into the soil. The tree's limbs were splayed across the top of the water like arms that had tried to stop its slide down the

muddy slope. Lori swam over and pulled off a mouthful of acorns. *Taste like peanuts,* she thought, grinding the shells between her teeth.

"Hey, wouldja look at that," a boy cried from the riverbank. "It's one of them manatees!"

Lori paused in her chewing to watch a boy about eleven years old scramble to his feet from where he had been prodding a caterpillar with a pine needle.

"Shhh." He gestured to a smaller fellow whose blonde head popped up from behind a stand of palmetto. "Watch me catch him."

"Billy, ya cain't catch no manatee," the younger boy said. "And if ya did, what wouldja do with him?"

"Just you be quiet and watch," Billy replied, kicking off his flipflops and eyeing Lori at the same time.

"I'm gonna tell Mom," little brother warned as big brother slid down the muddy slope.

"Will not."

"Will too!"

Billy eased into the river. The hems, then the knees of his jeans turned black in the cold water.

"Mom said the next time she caught ya messin' with one of those, she was gonna whip you good!"

"Well, Mom ain't here, and you ain't gonna tell her," Billy threatened through chattering teeth. "Now stay still and watch me ride him!" The boy stepped closer to Lori.

"But he's just a baby one," little brother cried.

"Yeah, but I bet he can still float me." Billy wriggled his short, stubby fingers at Lori. "Here, fishy fishy."

Like he really expects me to fall for that, Lori snorted.

The bubble delighted the boy. "See," Billy called to his

brother, "he likes me." The boy reached over to a branch and snapped it off. "Saw you eating these," he said, floating it in front of Lori. "You want some more acorns?"

Lori saw the gleam in the boy's eye and knew where this was going.

"Too slow!" Billy snatched the branch out of the water.

"Billy, why do ya have to be so mean," little brother wailed from the riverbank.

"Aw, I didn't mean it." Billy rested the branch back on the water, closer to his side. "I won't move it again, I promise."

Lori swam up; the boy lunged for her head.

Lori flicked her tail and backed quickly away. *Too slow yourself*, she thought.

Billy fell face first into the water. Furious, he sputtered to the surface. "Stupid animal!" He grabbed the branch and smashed it across Lori's back. "Eat this!"

The branch didn't hurt, but it made Lori angry. How many other manatees had Billy mistreated? She dove and charged the boy, her eighty pounds lifting him neatly off his feet. When Billy rose, wild-eyed, Lori spun and smacked him with her tail.

"Hey, ya ain't supposed to fight back," Billy whimpered, running comically through the waist-high water for the safety of the riverbank.

Lori charged again, this time squealing loudly.

Billy struggled up the slope. He fell and held his left hand up to his little brother. "Get me out of here!"

Little brother backed away, grinning.

Billy grabbed an empty soda can and launched it. The younger boy ducked. Billy grabbed a handful of rocks and stood to throw them at Lori. His bare feet slipped in the mud. He bit his tongue as he landed on the seat of his pants.

That'll show you, Lori thought, drowning out Billy's howls as she dove.

****

"That was very brave," a tiny voice said from under the oak. Lori squinted into the shadows. "What was?"

A catfish peeked out from between two branches. "That was." He twitched his whiskers toward the surface. "Taking on one of THEM."

"Yes it was, yes it was, yes it was!" the river repeated as marine life left the safety of the submerged trunk to talk to Lori.

"They like to hurt us!" A Redbelly water snake twisted to show where its tail had been cut off.

"And maim us!" A Speck opened its mouth, revealing a gash from a hook.

"And kill us," a Bluegill whispered.

"They won't leave my kind alone even though they know we're not fit to eat," a mudfish called up from the river bottom.

A Yellow-bellied slider eased his head from his shell. "Why should They have the right to plunder my nests?"

"Or gig my children?" croaked a bullfrog.

The turtle nipped at a minnow as it swam past. "Why can humans do what ever they want, and all we can do is get out of their way?"

"Or die trying?" The Bluegill shuddered.

"If we had more like *her*," a Warmouth nodded toward Lori,

105

"we could make them stop!"

A Golden shiner eyed the group unhappily. "Why can't we all just get along?"

"Because humans are baaad," a Sheephead answered.

"No they're not." An Alligator gar interrupted the conversation, swooping in from the channel. He looked down his long gray face at the group and announced, "It is because that's the way it always has been and that's the way it always shall be."

"Oh, why don't you go stick that in somebody else's business," the shiner said.

"Why don't you quit your carping?" The gar sneered, flashing his long rows of needlelike teeth at the tiny fish.

The shiner darted into a crack in a log. "If you had any brains, you'd see I ain't that kind of fish," he shouted once he was safely hidden.

"One breath created us, one breath animates us," the turtle mumbled, a water bug leg dangling from one side of his mouth.

"Yes, and that One decided long ago how it will be." The gar shrugged the best a fish can.

"But it isn't right," grumbled the Warmouth.

"It isn't fair," added the Redbellied snake.

Lori's lungs were burning. "Excuse me," she broke in, "I have to take a breath."

"Be careful, be careful, be careful!" the group called.

Lori surfaced. The riverbank was deserted.

"They're gone now," Lori assured her friends when she returned under water. "You will be okay for now."

"Yeah, you sure gave them a whoopin' ," the Warmouth cried. "We'll be safe now that you're here!"

"But I need to be on my way."

"What? Where?" the creatures asked.

"Oh, won't you stay," the mudfish begged with his bulging brown eyes. "I feel so much safer with you here."

"I'm on my way into the spring," Lori explained. "I want to find my parents."

"Humans ate mine," the Bluegill bubbled sadly.

"Then you can understand why it's so important that I be going."

"I'm headed to the great Blue Boil myself," said the Alligator gar. "Come along and I'll show you the way." With a swish, he was gone up river.

"Beware of the roar with the big shiny teeth," the catfish mewed, backing deeper into the tree limbs. "I've seen them chew up your kind."

Lori forced a smile, then turned and followed the gar.

"But Detective, you've got this all wrong," Mrs. Henderson said, slapping her palms on the long table in front of her. "Glenda and I have nothing to do with Joe Simpson's disappearance."

The detective rose from his seat and shut the door. "It's not Miss Hayes we're interested in Mrs. Henderson, it's you."

The woman looked up at him sharply.

"We've got it from numerous witnesses that you were seen arguing with Mr. Simpson out on the water yesterday afternoon. That during the course of your disagreement, you rammed his Jetski with your boat. Last night he didn't show up for his nine o'clock poker game." The man consulted his notes. "At midnight, Officer Barker reported you were behaving strangely at the municipal boat ramp. At 1:30 a.m., you're discovered dumping something heavy off your boat at Blue Spring. Today we find this."

He tossed a large plastic bag on the table and nudged it with his pencil eraser. Inside was Joe Simpson's sodden toupee. "Can you see why the police would want to talk to you?"

"Everybody hated him!" Mrs. Henderson glared at the mirror hanging behind the detective's head. She had seen enough

108

shows on TV to realize that behind it sat another member of law enforcement, listening. "Besides, our feud has gone on since we were kids. If I wanted to get rid of Joe, don't you think I would've done it sooner?"

"Maybe the opportunity never presented itself before."

Mrs. Henderson chewed the inside of her lip. As happy as it would have made her for old man Simpson to move away, she never wished him any harm. After the way she had tried to run him over, though, she'd have a hard time convincing a jury of that. She had to get herself off the hook, and in a hurry—Lori was out there in the water, alone!

"Mrs. Henderson?" the detective repeated.

The woman brought her thoughts back into the interrogation room. "You said something?"

"I said I wanted to know what you were doing yesterday evening between the hours of seven o'clock and midnight."

Mrs. Henderson laughed.

"You think this is funny?" The detective rested his palms on the table and leaned over her.

Mrs. Henderson smiled crookedly up at him. "You wouldn't believe me if I told you."

"Try me."

She shook her head. "You'd lock me up in the looney bin if I did."

"I could lock you up in jail if you don't."

Mrs. Henderson sat quietly for a moment. "Let me talk to Officer Barker," she finally said.

Lori hovered over a submerged log, her whiskers twitching. Though there was nothing to see, she could tell from odors left there that manatees of all shapes and sizes had recently passed by. The current, propelled by millions of gallons of water streaming from the spring, was definitely pushing harder here. *It'll be nice having that work for us on the way home,* she thought.

The Alligator gar doubled back to find her. "That's one of their message centers," he explained, nodding toward the log.

"Too bad I don't know how to use it," Lori said sadly. "I feel like I'm running out of time.

"We haven't much further to go," the gar replied. "Come along—let's find those parents of yours."

A group of manatees rested across the mouth of the spring.

"Thank you, oh thank you," Lori called to the gar.

The fish flashed his toothy grin and was gone.

Lori found herself in manatee gridlock. "Excuse me," she apologized as she inched through the bodies.

Progress was slow—manatees were swimming above her, others dozed on their backs below her. They were three-deep in some places. Lori thought of the saying "There's no such thing as too much of a good thing." In this case, it was wrong. How was she going to pick her parents out of this crowd?

Her lungs were burning; Lori surfaced to breathe. *Maybe I*

can search for them better from up here, she thought, craning her head as far as she could. All she saw was a sea of wrinkled gray skin. "Mom?" she called.

A puff of air answered to her right.

"Excuse me, excuse me," Lori nosed her way over. A large manatee blocked her path. Lori dove under it and resurfaced on the other side. "Dad? It's me, Lori!"

Again, she heard a puff.

Lori swam up to the manatee. She squinted into its face. "Mom?"

"Aaaaacho!" the animal sneezed into the water. "Forgib be, I seeb to hab cod a code."

"A code?" Lori looked into the animal's red, runny eyes. "Oh, a *cold.* So you weren't answering me when I was calling for my parents, were you?"

"I'b afraid dot." The manatee looked sorrowfully at Lori.

Lori's heart sank. It could take her three days to speak to each of the animals. By then she would have run out of time to return to the Portal. She could be trapped as a manatee for years!

"Perhaps I can be of assistance?" a familiar voice called from the sky.

"Maurice!"

The bird settled onto the water beside her. "In the feathers."

"How'd you know where to find me?"

"Have you forgotten where I sleep?" He turned his beak up and laughed. "What a sight that was—your grandmother barreling down the boardwalk trying to get you out of the Portal, and there you were, midway through the transformation. The way she stared at your tail—I nearly fell off my perch!"

"Yeah, that was pretty funny, wasn't it?" Lori smiled. "But Maurice, what do I do now? There are tons of manatees here."

"Literally," the seagull agreed.

"I could use up all my time just trying to find my parents."

"Now, now, never fear. I wouldn't have made the flight if hadn't already thought of that. Matter of fact," Maurice examined his reflection proudly, "not only do I know where your mother is, I also happen to know which one your mother is."

"Oh, take me to her, won't you?"

"It would be my pleasure," the bird said solemnly. "Follow me."

Maurice left Lori and flew low over the water. "She's over here," he called, circling the eastern side of the lagoon.

Lori eased through the herd as quickly as she could. She found Maurice perched on the guardrail at the ob-servation deck. He nodded toward a lone manatee dozing on the surface in a pool of sunshine.

"Mom?"

The manatee's whiskers twitched.

"Mom, it's me, Lori."

The female manatee's eyes shot open. "Lori?" She looked up at the empty observation deck.

"Over here."

Mrs. Sweeney gasped. "Lori, is it really you?"

"Is that really *you*?" Lori laughed, swimming up and look-ing deeply into the other animal's face.

Her mother's eyes filled with tears. "How did you get here?"

"I swam."

Mrs. Sweeney shook her head. "I mean how did you get *here* as a manatee?"

"You and Dad led me to the Portal."

"We did?"

"Yeah, remember a few months ago when Dad called for me? I heard him while I was out at Indian Point. His voice led me to the boardwalk, and I fell through the railing onto the Portal. Where is he, anyway? I can't wait to see him."

Mrs. Sweeney sighed. Lori was shocked to see how thin her mother had grown since the field trip.

"Mom, where's Dad? I've come to take you guys home."

Mrs. Sweeney closed her eyes. "He's not here."

"Well, tell me where he is and I'll go get him."

Mrs. Sweeney remained silent.

"Mom, I have two and a half days to get you and Dad home. C'mon, let's get him and get out of here!"

Mrs. Sweeney opened her eyes. "That night you found the Portal—" she paused.

"Yeah...."

"Was the night your father died."

"*What?*"

"We were in the channel over by the message log, thinking about you, talking about you, when a boat came speeding through the protected zone. It struck him." Mrs. Sweeney's voice broke. "He cried out your name one last time before he drowned."

Lori squeezed her eyes shut. She wanted to blot out the sun, her mother's grief, and the image she had of her father's last moments. She whispered, "If you already knew about the Portal, why didn't you come back through it?"

"We didn't know how it worked," Mrs. Sweeney moaned. "After *The Love Machine* swamped us and we fell in and transformed, we went back to Indian Point time and again to look for it. But it was never there."

Lori's stomach lurched—so this was all Joe Simpson's fault! If that horrible man hadn't been out driving his boat recklessly, none of this would have happened! The world around Lori turned red as she recalled the pain her family had suffered over the past three years. And all because of HIM!

She swallowed hard, burying her rage in her belly—she'd take care of Joe Simpson later. Right now she had to take care of her mother. "We'll leave this afternoon when the river is warmest," Lori said firmly. "I'm getting you home before it's too late."

"It's lucky for you the scuba divers didn't find anything," Officer Barker said as he escorted Mrs. Henderson down the corridor and out the front door of the police station.

"I told 'em the same thing I told you—I wasn't anywhere near Joe Simpson last night."

"Yes, but you never explained what you *were* doing," Officer Barker observed. "As a reminder, Nancy, you've only been released so you can go to work and home. Under no circumstances are you to leave town without notifying us first. Is that clear?"

"Loud and clear." Mrs. Henderson saluted sarcastically. They paused beside his patrol car. "No thanks," she said as Office Barker reached out to open the passenger door. "I'm headed straight to work."

"No tricks, Nancy?"

"Cross my heart."

The woman made a big show across her chest with her right hand, and crossed the fingers on her left tightly behind her back.

Lori spent the morning urging her mother to eat as much hydrilla and water lettuce as they could find. Mrs. Sweeney had grown gaunt while she mourned the loss of her husband. Lori gently praised each mouthful. "Now, why don't you take a nap," she said. "Maurice will tell us when it's time to leave."

"Lori, go on without me. I'm so weak I'll slow you down. Don't risk getting trapped."

"We'll be fine," Lori said. "Besides, I need you to show me the shortcuts."

Mrs. Sweeney caressed her daughter with her flipper. "I've looked for your face in every group of children. I've listened for your voice in every conversation. I can't believe you found me."

"Rest now, Mom, then we'll eat another bite before we head out."

"I'm afraid to close my eyes," Mrs. Sweeney said. "If this is only a dream and I wake up to find you gone, I won't survive it."

"I'll be right here, I promise." Lori rested her muzzle against her mother's side. Mrs. Sweeney's breaths became deeper. She sank, contentedly, to a sunny spot on the sandy bottom.

"Go ahead and get some shut-eye yourself, young lady,"

Maurice said. "You're going to need all your strength for the trip back.

"You'll let us know when it's time?"

"To the second," Maurice replied.

Lori yawned and joined her mother.

****

"It's time," Maurice called down into the water.

Lori stretched and rose to the surface for a breath. Her mother was still resting. Lori grabbed a bite of hydrilla before nudging her awake.

"I had the nicest dream." Mrs. Sweeney smiled. "We were at Indian Point having a picnic like we used to. Remember those, Lori, when we'd spread a quilt out under that old orange tree? Remember how, when the tree was in bloom, everything smelled so sweet?"

Lori nodded.

"In my dream, your dad had just seen two manatees swim by the end of the boardwalk. He called to us to come look..." Mrs. Sweeney stopped. "He's gone now."

"I know, Mom, and I miss him now more than I have the past three years. But I'm here with you, and it's time for us to leave. Grandmama's waiting."

Mrs. Sweeney looked over to the right. "There's somebody I need to say goodbye to."

Lori followed her mother. They stopped beside a large female manatee. A crescent-shaped scar ran across the top of the animal's head. Something about that scar was familiar.

"I want you to meet Amanda," Mrs. Sweeney said. "She adopted your father and me when we first transformed. We would have perished without her. Amanda, dear, this is my daughter, Lori. She's come to take me home."

The manatee's eyes grew soft. "Home," she echoed. "I used to dream about going home."

"Where are you from?" Lori asked.

Amanda smiled. "Oh, from a land far, far away."

"Can't you go back?"

"Nobody's there now," Amanda replied. "My parents are gone—all my sisters are, too."

"I'm sorry," Lori said.

Maurice coughed discreetly into his wing—they needed to be going.

"Well, thank you for taking such good care of my parents." Lori turned to leave.

"Be careful," Amanda said. "Wish I could join you simply for the adventure, but ever since I got this," she pointed to her head, "I've been afraid to leave the spring."

Lori stopped. Now she knew why the scar looked familiar— this was Dolly, the manatee Ranger Hartley had told them about in science class. And *she* had saved Lori's parents!

"I've heard about you," Lori said. "A park ranger told us how you let some boaters cut fishing line off of your flippers."

"Yes, that happened the last time I ventured out to see my sister."

"But I thought you said they were all..." Lori didn't want to finish her sentence.

"Yes, they are all gone, except the littlest who never transformed. She must have moved away. Glenda is the only one of us who was able to avoid the Portal."

"Glenda?" Lori squeaked. "Amanda?" She shook her head.

"You're Amanda *Hayes*? *The* Amanda Hayes who disappeared March 31, 1979? Miss Glenda's *sister*?"

The manatee nodded.

"Then you *have* to come home with us. Miss Glenda will... This will be the greatest... I can't wait to see her face when..."

"Lori, look at me," Amanda said. "I'm too old and too fat to make the trip. Even if I were ten years younger."

"But—"

"Tell Glenda that Amanda asked about her. Tell her I send my love."

"But—"

"I would only slow you down," Amanda said firmly. "Come back here and visit me after you've transformed. Promise me that, will you Lori?"

"Yes, but—"

"And bring Glenda. I'll be right here, waiting."

Maurice called from the sky. Lori and her mother left Amanda, and navigated through the dozing herd.

The current pushed the manatees past Blue Spring Landing. The two stayed close to shore where they were less likely to encounter boaters. Though it was January, there were plenty of people out on the water taking advantage of the mild, sunny day. At Stark's Cutoff, the river widened. Lori and her mother ate one last bite of ribbon grass before turning toward Lake Beresford.

The river grew darker the further they swam from the spring. By the evening of day one, they could see the city lights of Jacksonville. The manatees sank, exhausted, into the shallows to rest. Lori huddled next to her mother for warmth.

Wah-wah-wah. The whine of a speedboat closing in jolted Lori awake. She hurried over to her mother. Though the two were keeping to the shallows, they were still in danger of being hit. "Dive!" she squealed, swimming on top of the larger animal. Mrs. Sweeney sank into the mud. The water began vibrating. Lori pushed their bodies deeper into the soft river bottom, but her back remained just below the surface. An angry roar filled her ears. Lori tried not to think about the boat's sharp propellers shredding everything in their path at a rate of 1000 revolutions per minute. If she was lucky, she'd end up with a gash like Amanda's. If not... Lori refused think about it. Whatever it took, she would protect her mother.

Her bones began to shudder.

She braced herself for the collision.

"Hey," a man shouted from the bow. "Watch out!"

Though the boat swerved away, Lori wasn't safe—the propellers could still catch her.

She squeezed her eyes shut. The prop wash yanked her off her mother and tossed her about in the wake.

When Lori twisted herself around, her mother was gone. She had to wait for the sound of the engines to fade away before she could cry out. "Mom! Where are you?" There she was, twenty feet away, burrowed into the marsh grass. Lori swam over. "Mom, are you okay?"

Mrs. Sweeney was too frightened to answer. She whimpered when Lori ran a flipper across her back.

"It's okay," Lori murmured as she nuzzled the trembling body. But was it? The water was so thick with mud she couldn't see if her mother had been injured. "C'mon, let's get out of here."

Mrs. Sweeney wept softly. "Oh, Lori, I can't."

"We *have* to," Lori said. "We're not safe here. We've gotta get down river before another boat comes."

Reluctantly Mrs. Sweeney left the marsh grass. The two manatees swam together in silence, both alert for the faintest warning of more boats. After an hour, Lori discovered a narrow stream branching off the river where the water was shallow and warm. Lori and her mother grazed on turtle grass and dozed in the sunshine.

****

"Lori, time to get up," a little voice said in her ear.

Lori stuck her head under water.

Something landed on her back. Something with sharp claws. Lori rolled over to wash whatever that something was off.

"Lori, you must be moving on!"

"Maurice," Lori grumbled, "come back in twenty minutes."

"You don't have twenty minutes to waste," the seagull squawked. "Another extended vacation like the one you have just taken, and you and your mother will never reach the Portal in time!"

Lori looked at the sky. The sun was setting—no wonder

she was cold. And the cold made it hard to think. "Where are we?"

"A mile or so south of Saint Augustine. If my calculations are correct, you must average a speed of 7.8 miles per hour from this point on if you are to reach the Portal before the end of this Blue Moon."

"Don't get your feathers in a wad," Lori said. "There's plenty of time left—we've got a whole other day."

"No you don't, you have slept nearly twenty-four hours." The bird looked at her sharply. "Don't you realize that?"

Lori shook her head. Her thoughts were tangled up in seaweed.

"I should have wakened you sooner," Maurice cried, "but your mother seemed desperate for rest."

"Where is she?"

"Over there," the bird pointed over his shoulder with his beak.

Lori swam to her mother and nudged her awake. "Mom. Mom, it's time to go."

Mrs. Sweeney groaned.

"Mom, are you okay?"

"Yes," the manatee whispered. "Just so very tired."

"I know," Lori said. "Me too. It's this cold water—hypothermia is setting in. But we've gotta keep moving." Her stomach rumbled. "Let's swim into the channel and find something to eat."

The stars were beginning to stand out from the graying sky as Lori and her mother moved painfully into the wider, even cooler, water. Hydrilla grew thickly in this part of the Intercoastal Waterway, and the two were able to graze and swim at the same time. The moon, glowing white on the horizon, lit their way, its rays mingled with mist rising from the river's surface.

It started to rain. Hard, cold drops pelted the weary animals pushing southward against the current. Lori and her mother rested briefly in the shelter of a low bridge. The clouds broke.

"Maurice, I need you to fly to Miss Glenda's kitchen window and tap on it. That's our signal."

"Ah." Maurice nodded. "Like that poem by Edgar Allen Poe. 'Once upon a midnight dreary—'"

"Not you, too," Lori moaned. "Just go!"

The seagull set off. Lori heard a cackle and a weak "Nevermooooore" as he disappeared into the night.

"Maurice!" Miss Glenda threw open her kitchen door. "Nancy. Nancy!" She elbowed the dozing woman. "It's time! He's here!"

Mrs. Henderson grabbed her keys from the table and followed Miss Glenda out the door and down to the boathouse. She looked over the water. "There's nobody there."

Maurice squawked from the boathouse roof.

"Are you sure that's the right bird?"

Miss Glenda looked from the river to the bird. "I've never met him... But I've never had one tap on my window before, either."

Maurice swooped off his perch. He flew a short distance upriver. *They're this way!*

"Maybe he bumped into your window by accident," Mrs. Henderson said, looking out over the water again. She yawned. "Well, I'm going back to the house. There's nobody out here and I'm not going to risk being down here when the real bird gets up *there*."

Maurice saw the woman was leaving. He flew across her path. Mrs. Henderson swatted him away and kept walking. Maurice made a loop and flew at her again, this time backing her towards the *Whoop-de-doo*.

"Nancy, I think he wants you to get in your boat."

"Of all the crazy notions," Mrs. Henderson said. "Lori told us she'd send the bird when they got here. They're not here.

This gull is probably just protecting its nest."

Maurice flew up to Mrs. Henderson a third time. When the woman raised her hand to bat him away, he nipped her keys out of her upraised hand, and dropped them with a *clink* into the bottom of the boat.

"I guess that settles that," Miss Glenda said, climbing in.

Mrs. Henderson shook her head and joined Miss Glenda. She tugged on the starting cord. The engine sputtered feebly. "It won't start!" She tugged the cord again. "It's out of gas. Do you have any?"

"Just what's in my car."

"Then stay right here." She grabbed her keys. " I'm going to run to the corner station—it's open all night."

Maurice squawked, *There isn't time!*

Mrs. Henderson climbed out onto the pier. "I won't be long."

The moon disappeared behind a cloud.

The wind began to gust.

"Oh my," Miss Glenda exclaimed, "I hope it isn't about to storm."

Mrs. Henderson hurried past the old orange tree.

"Wait," the leaves whispered.

The woman spun around and stared into the shadows. "Who said that?"

Silence.

She ran past the lily pond.

"Stop!" A bullfrog chugged.

"Who's there?"

Miss Glenda appeared by Mrs. Henderson's side. "What is it, Nancy? You look like you've seen a ghost."

Mrs. Henderson pulled her keys and wallet out of her jacket pocket. "I've gotta get out of this evil place!" She handed her things to Miss Glenda. "Take these and go get some gas for the boat. I'll be waiting for you in the house." She ran to the comfort of Miss Glenda's kitchen and slammed the door. She sat down at the kitchen table and poured out a cup of tepid tea.

Crash!

Mrs. Henderson stood and cracked open the kitchen door. Miss Glenda stood on the path, her long gray hair whipped about her head. "A tree limb, a big one—" she yelled, gesturing with her arms—"fell down right behind your truck. I can't get out! I ran back here because Nancy the wind has a message. And it's for you!"

Mrs. Henderson stepped out onto the landing. Miss Glenda hurried up to her.

"Must goooo," the trees around them moaned. "Must gooo!"

Miss Glenda gripped Mrs. Henderson's elbow. "So what do we do now?"

"Do?" Mrs. Henderson snapped as they followed the path to the parking lot. She looked at the fallen limb. "Can't drive to Lori—the truck's blocked. Can't get to her on the water—the boat won't start. What are we supposed to do, walk?"

Miss Glenda's eye had wandered across the gardens to Joe Simpson's home. "Not by land, nor sea," she said to herself, "but by AIR. Come on, Nancy, we'll fly there!"

"Like a little birdie?" Mrs. Henderson snorted. "Oh Glenda, you *are* nuts."

Miss Glenda grabbed Mrs. Henderson by the hand. "Like a great big, beautiful birdie," she announced, pushing open the gate into old man Simpson's back yard and pointing to his ultralight.

"I thought you said you could drive any kind of boat!"

Mrs. Henderson eyed the ultralight uneasily. "I said I can drive anything with a prop—*when* it's in the water."

"Then I'll do it," Miss Glenda said, shooing Mrs. Henderson forward. The inflatable raft rocked.

"No you won't!" Mrs. Henderson slapped Miss Glenda's hand off the tiller. "I've seen you drive my truck. Sit down there in the bottom of this confounded thing, and watch for Lori over the side."

Miss Glenda sat down in a huff. She held up a life jacket. "There's only one of these. You want it?"

"Nah, I don't need it," Mrs. Henderson said.

Miss Glenda sat on the life jacket. "Then I'll just keep it close by in case of emergency."

Mrs. Henderson pulled the starting cord. The prop whirred to life.

The backyard lights flashed on.

Miss Glenda ducked down. "Somebody's here," she whispered. "They've heard us!"

Moonlight glinted off the barrel of a shotgun. A man called from behind a palm tree, "I'm gonna give you one chance to stop what you're doing and get outta my boat!"

Mrs. Henderson shouted over the noisy propeller, "Joe Simpson, is that you? You've caused me a lot of trouble. You're supposed to be dead!"

"Well you just about killed me," he yelled back. "And look what you did to my Jetski." He pointed the shotgun

127

towards a large, tarp-covered lump, then back at the ultralight.

"Serves you right!" Mrs. Henderson squinted into the shadows. "Say, where *have* you been? The police picked me up for questioning the other night—said you'd been murdered because you didn't show up for your regular poker game."

"Well I couldn'ta gone like *this*," the man whined, stepping into the yard. His pale, bald head glowed under the bright lights. "Fellas never would've let me live it down. I slept in my car so nobody'd see." He peered down the sights on his shotgun. "Now get out of my ultralight before *I* face murder charges!"

"Joe Simpson, I'm not going anywhere except up-river. You're welcome to try to shoot me, but just remember, that buckshot is more apt to go through this gizmo of yours, than it is through me. So fire away" she said, revving the engine, "or get out of my way!"

The man backed toward his house. "I'm calling the police!"

"You do that," Mrs. Henderson called after him. "And while you're at it, tell 'em to bring you your hairpiece. It's in the evidence locker."

Mr. Simpson scurried away.

"Glenda," Mrs. Henderson announced, "cast off."

Maurice fluttered onto the bow of the raft.

"Hang onto your tail feathers," Miss Glenda whispered.

Maurice looked at her over his shoulder. Moonlight glinted off one glossy eye. It disappeared, then was back.

Did he just wink at me? Miss Glenda thought. "Nancy, did that bird just wink at me?"

Mrs. Henderson didn't answer—she was too busy twisting knobs.

Maurice cackled and hunched his neck down into his shoulders. *Ready for takeoff!*

The ultralight eased away from the dock. As the propeller hummed louder, the boat gathered speed. With a bump it left the water.

Lori's teeth were chattering. She searched the horizon for her grandmother's boat. The world was silent except for a light breeze rustling through the cat tails. She was tired, bone weary. Every inch of her body pleaded for rest, but Lori knew instinctively that it was not the thing to do. To fall asleep now would mean drowning. A buzzing filled her ears. She shook her head to clear them.

A dark shadow passed over the moon—a solid shadow blacker and thicker than any storm cloud she had ever seen. A piece of the shadow broke off and spiraled downward. Lori remembered her mysterious dream from long ago, and ducked under water. When she rose, the moon was clear.

"Where's your mother?" Maurice asked, floating over to Lori.

Lori could barely focus her eyes. She had begun dozing, and couldn't shake the sensation of dropping off to sleep.

Maurice fluttered his wings against her face. "Lori, look at me! Tell me where your mother is!"

"She was right here a minute ago," Lori replied thickly. "Tell you when I wake up."

"You'll do no such thing, young lady. Pull yourself together and help me find her!"

Lori sighed. Apparently she would not be allowed to resume her nap until Maurice was happy. "Last time I saw her was over there." She yawned and pointed limply to the east bank. "In those weeds. Now leave me alone."

Maurice found Mrs. Sweeney trembling in the shallows. *They're here! They're here!* He called to the ultralight. Mrs. Henderson heard his cry and adjusted their course. "Help's coming," he assured Mrs. Sweeney. "Your mother's here. Just a little bit longer and we'll have you and Lori safely at the Portal."

The ultralight dropped out of the sky like a lead-bellied pelican. Mrs. Henderson motored over to Lori. "Baby?" She reached out and caressed the wrinkled brow. "Is that you?"

Lori looked dreamily into her grandmother's face. She puffed a gentle greeting.

Maurice squawked from where he was floating next to Mrs. Sweeney. Mrs. Henderson sped over. "Margo?"

The large manatee stared silently.

Mrs. Henderson looked around. "Where's Jim?"

The manatee closed her eyes.

"Glenda, do you see another big manatee around here?" She craned her neck, looking up and down the shoreline. "I don't see him! Oh, what has happened?"

Miss Glenda looked at the listless animals. "Nancy, we've got to get these two out of here and fast."

"Maurice," Lori called, "go with Grandmama. Hurry! I don't know how much longer we can hold out!"

The seagull fluttered onto the ultralight. *"GO!"* He squawked.

"What am I supposed to do?" Mrs. Henderson asked.

"Maybe he wants you to take him somewhere," Miss Glenda replied.

"I'm not leaving my girls!"

"Then get out and wait here while I get some help."

"You don't know how to drive this thing!"

"I can do as good a job as you did," Miss Glenda replied, rocking the inflatable raft as she moved aft. "Besides, I was watching how you did it."

"GO!" Maurice repeated, flapping his wings frantically.

"All right." Mrs. Henderson climbed out of the raft into the waist-deep water. "Hurry, Glenda. They're nearly frozen!"

Miss Glenda spun the ultralight and sped down river.

"There they are!" Joe Simpson poked Officer Barker in the shoulder and pointed north.

The policeman aimed his high-powered flashlight at the bow of the approaching craft. "Looks like she's coming in."

The ultralight slowed near the pier. "What's that hanging off the bow?" the policeman asked. "A seagull?"

Miss Glenda winced in the bright light. She cupped her hands around her mouth. "We've got two manatees stranded on the other side of the Granada Bridge," she yelled. "Come help!"

Mr. Simpson ran to the end of the pier. "Get outta my ultralight!"

Miss Glenda spun the craft around. "Come on, I'll show you where!"

Mr. Simpson's threats were drowned out by the noisy propeller. Officer Barker pulled alongside him in his patrol boat. "You riding with me?"

Mr. Simpson sneered. "Not in that tug boat." He threw his shotgun into the bottom of *The Love Machine* and fired up its 350 horsepower engine. His pier vanished behind a thick wall of exhaust.

Miss Glenda looked behind her to see if the men were following. Maurice flapped his wings. "Are you sure?" she asked.

The seagull flapped harder. Miss Glenda pulled on the control stick. The raft bumped across the waves, then left the water.

****

Lori heard the approaching boats and watched the ultralight pass in front of the moon. "Help's coming, Mom!"

The Love Machine roared past. By the time its wake reached the shallows, the waves were angry and strong. Mrs. Henderson placed herself between the manatee and the seawall. Each time a wave crashed into them, the old woman pushed back, trying desperately to protect her daughter from the rocks.

Miss Glenda circled. She first pointed Lori out to Officer Barker then the two struggling in the surf. The policeman slowed his boat.

Mr. Simpson looked over his shoulder at the receding patrol boat. No one could catch *The Love Machine.* Ha ha! Because, he realized suddenly, *no one was trying.* He had overshot his destination! He spun the wheel and pushed forward on the throttle. Stupid manatees! It was all because of them that he was out here in the middle of the night, his head as bare as the day he was born, and his ultralight under the command of that crazy Glenda Hayes. He hunched over the steering wheel. It was time to put an end to this foolishness once and for all!

Officer Barker noted where Lori floated in the channel, then idled over to Mrs. Henderson. "Nancy, are you all right?"

"I'm fine, George," she said, wiping her eyes on her sleeve. "But these manatees are hurting."

Miss Glenda watched in horror as *The Love Machine* doubled-back. She screamed down to Officer Barker, "He's going to hit Lori!"

The policeman turned his boat north. "Stay here," he instructed Mrs. Henderson.

Miss Glenda looked from the speeding boat to the manatee. The distance between them was rapidly closing. She threw her weight to the right and aimed for *The Love Machine*. She set her jaw firmly. "You will not hurt her!"

Officer Barker motored into the channel, turned his patrol boat sideways in front of Lori, and cut the engine. He stood and gestured with his flashlight to guide the cabin cruiser around.

The ultralight dropped. Miss Glenda set her feet and pulled on the control stick with both hands. Mr. Simpson ducked as the craft skimmed his bow. Maurice turned around. *Bombs away!* He cackled, raising his tail. Miss Glenda soared back into the sky.

Joe Simpson wiped off his scalp while he fumbled by his feet for his shotgun. He loaded two shells into the chambers and snapped the barrel shut. *How sweet it's gonna be blasting that lunatic out of the air.* He thought. *Almost as sweet as it's gonna be presenting her with the repair bill.*

Officer Barker waved his flashlight.

She and that no-good Nancy Henderson. As soon as City Hall opens, I'm gonna march in and file charges for my Jetski and my ultralight. He grinned. *Maybe they'll throw Nancy in jail—then she'll have to close that stupid bait shack!*

"Watch out!" the policeman yelled.

Now, where is she? Mr. Simpson peered through the sights into the sky. A niggling thought made him look down. *And where was that patrol boat?*

134

Oh no!

He yanked the wheel. *The Love Machine* skipped across the top of the water. Officer Barker leaped out of the patrol boat into the river. The cigarette boat spun, collided with its own wake, soared briefly through the air, then landed hard, pitching Joe Simpson over board.

Officer Barker bobbed to the surface. With strong strokes, he swam to rescue Mr. Simpson.

The Love Machine careened across the river. It slammed into a dock and burst into flames.

Bits of debris rained down on Lori. She snapped awake. "Mom?"

"Here!" Maurice answered from the shallows.

Lori swam over. "Are you okay?"

"Cold," the older manatee mumbled. "So cold."

Lori nudged her mother. "The Portal is just around the bend. See the lights on the Granada Bridge? We're nearly there. Come on, Mom, just a little bit further!"

Mrs. Sweeney roused herself. With a mighty effort she followed Lori. Mrs. Henderson trailed behind. The trio moved silently in the wail of sirens, the fire and the full moon lighting their way.

Miss Glenda was waiting at Indian Point. Mrs. Henderson went with her into the boathouse to retrieve the rope ladder. Lori left her mother's side and dove. Her transformation began as Officer Barker ran up the boardwalk. "Stop what you're doing, right there," he ordered.

"We can't, George," Mrs. Henderson replied. "This is a matter of life and death."

Joe Simpson was three steps behind the policeman. He pointed furiously to the ultralight then to the women. "What are you waiting for, Officer? Arrest them!"

"Nancy," Officer Barker began, "I'm not asking you, I'm telling you. Come away from the water."

"George, look at me—look at *this*," Mrs. Henderson said, pointing down to Lori and the manatee floating listlessly by her side.

"Grandmama," Lori called up to the boardwalk, "Mom's too weak to swim any further. I need some help!"

"Lori," Officer Barker said, "where did you come from?"

"I've been out here trying to help this manatee!"

"I've already radioed that in to the wildlife center. They're sending a team now."

"But that's not what she needs. She needs us!"

"Nancy," the officer looked at Mrs. Henderson. "I'm not going to stand here arguing with you. Get your things and come with me."

"Lori," Mrs. Henderson spoke softly. "You got anything to show him?"

Lori nodded.

"George, take a look at the girl."

Lori floated onto her back and flipped her tail into the air.

"What sort of a game is this?" Joe Simpson snorted.

"It's not a game, it's deadly serious," Mrs. Henderson snapped. She turned to the dumbstruck policeman. "Give us five minutes and you'll know everything."

"In five minutes I plan to be drinking a hot cup of coffee. Maybe with a shot of whiskey in it," the officer mumbled, rubbing his forehead.

"George, I'm asking you to believe me."

"You're asking me to lose my job!"

"Give us five more minutes, then you can arrest us if you want. But George, please, I'm begging you, give us those five minutes."

"I'll need help holding her head down," Lori called to the officer. "Mr. Simpson, I'll need you, too."

Officer Barker pulled off his soggy socks and shoes. He unbuckled his belt, then looked around for a place to put his gun and identification. With a shake of his head, he handed his belongings to Miss Glenda.

"Don't touch the sand where it's glowing," Lori cautioned.

The officer tapped the face of his wristwatch. "Five minutes, starting now," he said, trotting down the boardwalk.

Joe Simpson wrapped himself in one of Mrs. Henderson's towels and leaned against the boathouse.

"Hurry," Lori pleaded, "or she'll drown!"

The man shook his head and smirked at the officer wading through the cold water.

"This is all your fault, do you know that?" Lori screamed. "It was *your* boat that waked my parents three years ago. They never would have fallen onto the Portal if it hadn't been for *you*. Because of you my father's dead!"

Mr. Simpson's smirk froze.

"Grandmama, I'm gonna change back so I can talk to Mom. Miss Glenda, call 911 and have them send an ambulance."

Mrs. Henderson tore her eyes away from Joe Simpson. "Don't do it, Lori!"

"Honey, look at the horizon, there isn't time," Miss Glenda cried.

"It's the only way to make sure Mom survives the transformation," Lori said. "I didn't bring her here for you to watch her die." The girl looked from the horizon, glowing pink, to her mother. "I've got plenty of time," she lied.

Officer Barker stepped around the Portal.

"I'm going to lead her to you," Lori explained. "After that, help me get her head down."

Lori dove. The transformation came quickly. She swam to her mother. "Mom, Mom, it's me, Mom, Lori. We're here to go through the Portal, remember?"

"Lori?" her mother mumbled. "I can't find my Lori and she can't find me.""

"Yes you did, Mom, see? I'm right here. We're both at the Portal, and look, look up there—Grandmama's waiting for us!"

"Can't see," her mother murmured. "Can't see anything."

"Then I'll guide you." Lori nudged her mother gently in the side. "Swim that way."

The large manatee did not respond.

"Mom?"

Her tail began to sink.

"Mom!"

Joe Simpson pushed his hands against his ears to block out the calf's pitiful squeals. He turned and started down the boardwalk. Nancy Henderson was right behind him. "Do something!" she yelled. Mr. Simpson broke into a run. He dashed across the parking lot and pushed open his gate. At his back door he pulled out his house key, but his shaking hands wouldn't let him thread it into the lock. Mrs. Henderson snatched the keyring out of his fingers and threw it into the trees. "Do something," she repeated, spinning Mr. Simpson around and shoving him toward the river. "This is all (push) your (push) fault!"

Officer Barker called from the water, "Come on! I can't do this by myself!"

"Mom, listen to me, help is here," Lori spoke urgently into her mother's ear. "We're gonna get you out of the water. All I need you to do is take a deep breath. Make it the biggest you can. Officer Barker is helping me guide you to the Portal. I'll be here with you the whole time, okay, so don't be afraid. Just one deep breath, you hear me? Just one big, deep breath and you'll be fine." Lori rubbed her muzzle against her mother's side.

There was no response.

"Mom, let me see you do it, then we're done. One deep breath and you're out of here!"

The larger manatee sighed.

"No!" Lori placed her muzzle against her mother's cheek. "Just one breath, Mom." She exhaled gently across her mother's nostrils. "A big one, like this."

Mrs. Sweeney trembled as the warm air caressed her face. Her eyes opened. She stared at the young manatee.

"Like this, Mom, like this." Lori exhaled again.

Mrs. Sweeney breathed in her daughter's sweet breath. Her body quit trembling, her tail rose.

"Good," Lori said. "Now hold it, and don't be afraid. Officer Barker and I are going to guide you to the Portal."

The policeman pressed carefully on the manatee's head. She remained on the surface. "Hurry up Simpson," he called to the man lingering in the shallows. "Help me before we lose her!"

Mr. Simpson waded reluctantly in, and both men pushed against the animal's head. The weak creature submitted to the pressure.

Lori dove. "Almost there, Mom. Keep holding your breath. Don't let it out yet."

The Portal bathed the manatee in a golden light. With a surge of renewed strength, Mrs. Sweeney flipped her tail and positioned herself head-down in the silt.

Lori watched the transformation in awe: first her mother's skin turned pink, then her neck and ears emerged. Her nose straightened. Mrs. Sweeney struggled as she began choking. The men, standing above her, couldn't see that the transformation had taken place. They thought the manatee was trying to remain in position and continued holding her under water.

"She's drowning!" Lori squealed, ramming the men and setting her mother free.

Mrs. Sweeney floated unconscious to the surface.

Officer Barker caught the woman's head and shoulders. "Grab her legs, Simpson!"

"But she doesn't have any," the man whispered as he slid

his arms under the gray torso.

"Throw me a blanket," Officer Barker called up to Mrs. Henderson. "I'll carry her out."

"No, no, you can't do that!" Miss Glenda tied a loop in the rope ladder before lowering it. "She has to come straight out of the Portal for the transformation to be complete."

"That's ridiculous," Officer Barker scoffed.

"We didn't make the rules," Mrs. Henderson said, tossing him a blanket. The rest of her words were drowned out by the harsh shrill of the ambulance.

The policeman quickly bundled Mrs. Sweeney, then threaded the rope under her arms. He jerked his thumb upwards for Mrs. Henderson and Miss Glenda to pull her onto the boardwalk.

Mrs. Henderson wept as she wiped her daughter's hair off her forehead. She placed her cheek against the cold face. "You're home again, Margo. Safe now. Safe at home," she murmured. "You and Lori and me, we're all together again. Lori!" Mrs. Henderson shouted. "Hurry up girl, and get out of that water!"

There was no answer.

"Glenda, where's Lori? Where's my girl?"

Maurice flew off the boathouse roof and landed on the concrete manatee. He cocked his head and looked at the water.

"Officer Barker, did you help her get out?" Glenda asked when he joined them on the boardwalk. The man shook his head. "Then she's still in the river!" Glenda kicked off her shoes. She leaped off the dock into the water.

The sun broke the horizon.

The seagull shrieked.

The girl was gone.

Lori had transformed, but her energy was spent and her lungs were empty of air. She lay limply on the river bottom, being pushed and pulled by the waves until the current picked her up and carried her to the end of the pier. Her father was there, motioning her to come closer.

"Daddy, what are you doing here?"

"Come see the manatees," he called.

Lori laid her sandwich down on the old quilt and rose to her feet. She felt light as a moonbeam and floated over the splintery boards to join him.

****

"Let me go!" Mrs. Henderson begged, struggling against the policeman's restraining arms. "Let me go!"

****

"Any sign of her?" Mr. Simpson called to Officer Barker.

****

Miss Glenda groped the black water blindly. Her lungs

felt like they were going to burst. She rose for a quick breath.

****

Maurice squawked as if his heart would break. *"Where is the girl? Where is the girl?"* He cried over and over again.

****

"Where's Glenda?" Mrs. Henderson yelled. "Anybody see her? Last time she came up was over a minute ago!"

****

The current carried Miss Glenda past the concrete manatee. *Maybe,* she thought, *it brought Lori this way, too!* She forced her body to hang limply. Her eyes struggled to see through the silt.

****

"Aren't they beautiful?" Mr. Sweeney said. "Come closer, Lori, so you can see them better."

****

Miss Glenda's lungs were burning, but she refused to rise to the surface. Too much valuable time was being wasted bobbing up and down. She closed her eyes, no longer trying to see through the water, but rather to *feel* her way. With a sense of desperation, she realized she would only be able to remain submerged another few seconds.

****

Mr. Sweeney held out his hand. "Hold onto me, Lori, the railing is rotten in places."

Lori reached out. Her father grabbed her wrist. His skin was wet—his flesh was icy cold.

Lori tried to pull away; Mr. Sweeney tightened his grip.

Lori twisted and turned her arm, struggling to break free, but her father was too strong! She reached across with her right hand and plucked at his fingers. His other hand clamped down on her. Now both of Lori's hands were caught!

He yanked upwards.

****

Miss Glenda shot to the surface. "I've got her!" She dove again and pulled Lori to the air. "Get the ladder!"

Mrs. Henderson broke free from Officer Barker and leaped into the river. The two women pulled Lori to the rope. Officer Barker raised her onto the pier. "She's not breathing!" he called to the Emergency Medical Technician.

The EMT left Mrs. Sweeney's stretcher and bent over Lori. He cleared her airway, then placed the plastic respirator over her nose and mouth.

"Lori?" her mother cried weakly. "Baby?"

The EMT squeezed the bulb.

"Lori, you need to take a deep breath," Mrs. Sweeney called over the EMT's shoulder. "Make it the biggest you can."

The EMT squeezed the respirator again.

"Lori, just one breath," her mother pleaded from her stretcher.

The girl lay still.

The EMT checked her pulse. "She's gone."

"No she isn't!" Mrs. Sweeney crawled off her stretcher and across the rough boards to her daughter's side. "She just can't hear me, isn't that right?" Mrs. Sweeney caressed Lori's forehead and whispered into her ear. "Baby, it's me, Mom. I need you to breathe for me, okay?" She blew softly across her child's face. "Like this—" Mrs. Sweeney pressed her mouth against Lori's and exhaled forcefully. She looked hopefully up at the EMT. "Did her eyelid move?"

The EMT shook his head. How he hated this part of his job!

Mrs. Sweeney exhaled again into her daughter's lungs. Pulling away, she repeated Lori's words, "One big, deep breath and you'll be fine."

Lori felt warm all over.

****

Her father smiled.

****

Lori coughed; the EMT rolled her onto her side.

****

Mr. Sweeney raised his right hand.

****

Lori filled her lungs deeply, gratefully with the crisp morning air.

****

Mr. Sweeney waved goodbye.

Epilogue

Mrs. Sweeney will be released from the hospital today. Lori stood at the top of the Granada Bridge looking out over the water. The Halifax River was unusually calm—perfectly smooth except where a school of mullet darted left and right just below the surface. Lori leaned over the guardrail and watched the faint lines melt into the water. The morning sun reflected up into her face, forcing her to close her eyes. A yellow ball glowed beneath her lids—it wasn't unpleasant, she'd just have to wait a moment for it to fade.

While she waited, she listened. All was still. There was a sense of expectancy in the air. Then it came—the same puff of life God breathed into Adam, the same breath that revived Lori and her mother. The earth stirred and yawned. A soft breeze, like a contented sigh, ruffled her hair.

Lori opened her eyes. The water had broken into shiny wrinkles. She tossed a handful of crumbs to Maurice wheeling over her head, then turned her bike toward home.

Florida Manatee Sanctuary Act
Chapter 68C-22, F.A.C.

... "it is unlawful for any person at any time, by any means, or in any manner intentionally or negligently to annoy, molest, harass, or disturb or attempt to molest, harass, or disturb any manatee; injure or harm or attempt to injure or harm any manatee; capture or collect or attempt to capture or collect any manatee; pursue, hunt, wound, kill or attempt to pursue, hunt, wound, or kill any manatee; or possess, literally or constructively, any manatee or any part of any manatee."

What do you do if you see a manatee that is dead, injured, or one that is being bothered?

Please call the **Florida Fish and Wildlife Marine Conservation Commission Marine Law Enforcement Unit**

>   1-888-404-FWCC (3922)
>   *or* *FWC on your cell
>   *or* use VHF Channel 16 on your marine radio

For additional information about Manatees,
write or call:

**Florida Fish and Wildlife
Conservation Commission**
Habitat and Species Conservation
Imperiled Species Management
620 South Meridian Street, HSC-ISM
Tallahassee, FL 32399-1600
(850) 922-4330
www.MyFWC.com/psm

Save the Manatee Club
500 N. Maitland Ave.
Maitland, FL 32751
(800) 432-JOIN (5646)
Free education packets are available for students.
Educator's guides and posters are available for teachers
and homeschoolers.
www.savethemanatee.org

TO SEE MANATEES IN CAPTIVITY:

Disney's Epcot Center
(407) 824-4321
Orlando, FL
*Manatees are found at the Living Seas exhibit.
Entry fee required*

SeaWorld
www.seaworld.org

Homosassa Springs Wildlife State Park
(352) 628-5343

Homosassa Springs, FL

Educational programs are presented each day by park staff.
Entrance fee required

Lowry Park Zoo
(813) 932-0245

Tampa, FL

This is a manatee rehabilitation facility.
Entrance fee required

Miami Seaquarium
(305) 361-5705

Miami, FL

This is a manatee rehabilitation facility.
Entrance fee required

Mote Marine Laboratory and Aquarium
(941) 388-2451

Sarasota, FL

Mote Marine Lab has two manatees and numerous other aquatic
wildlife at their research facility.
Entrance fee required

SeaWorld of Florida
(407) 363-2613

Orlando, FL

This is a manatee rehabilitation facility.
Theme park manatee program.
Entrance fee required

South Florida Museum
(941) 746-4131

Bradenton, FL

Parker Manatee Aquarium is home to Snooty, the oldest captive
manatee in Florida.
Entrance fee required

Blue Spring State Park
(386) 775-3663
Orange City, FL
*The park schedules manatee programs throughout
the day.*
Entry fee required

Moore's Creek—Ft. Pierce Utilities Authority
(772) 466-1600 ext.3333
Ft. Pierce, FL
*Manatees may be viewed from the Manatee Observation
and Education Center near the discharge canal.*

Orange River and FPL Discharge Canal
State Road 80
Fort Meyers, FL
*The Lee County Manatee Park has volunteers
available at the discharge canal viewing area.*
Parking fee. Gates close at 5pm

Tampa Bay—Tampa Electric Company
Manatee Viewing Center
(813) 228-4289
Ruskin, FL
Visitor Center, overlook and walkway.

To see these viewing areas on-line, log onto
 www.savethemanatee.org/places.htm

"There are several organizations dedicated to protecting manatees, and they have very informative web sites. Remember though, it is up to you, the boater, to respect the manatee zones. It is up to you, the fisherman, to dispose of your fishing line and litter properly. And, finally, it is up to you, as the parents of our future generations, to respect wildlife so that one day *your* children can watch these animals swimming in the wild."

FLORIDA PARK RANGER, WAYNE HARTLEY

The Artists

Frank Ritchie, Jr. (Cover)

A native of New York, Mr. Ritchie is known for pointillism, an impressionist style of painting where each "point" of color is carefully placed to create his magical landscapes. "You have to step back to see it," he says. "I walk back ten feet, then come up and put one dot here and one dot there and try to imagine."

Painting is a comfort to Mr. Ritchie, who has suffered from schizophrenia since his 30's. The National Association for Research on Schizophrenia and Depression has chosen several of his works to be printed on note cards and a holiday card. "All of them have been very popular," NARSAD co-founder Hal Hollister said. "The holiday card 'Silverscape' (created by Mr. Ritchie) I think is one of the best we've ever done."

JoAnne Thorn (Interior Illustrations)

Mrs. Thorn is an artist of many media: ceramics, photography, acrylic paints, and graphic design. For the past 15 years she has explored the creative possibilities of combining digital photography with freehand drawing and painting. She, her husband Mike, and their daughter Michelle, live less than a mile from Blue Spring Park.

JoAnne's work has been exhibited at the Daytona Beach Museum of Arts and Science, at Epcot, and at the Orlando Museum of Art's "Art and Technology Show." One of her manatee paintings won first, second *and* third places in the 2000-2001 Florida Fish and Wildlife Conservation Manatee Decal Competition.

Both Mrs. Thorn and Mr. Ritchie are members of **Very Special Arts** of Volusia. VSAV is a nonprofit affiliate of the John F. Kennedy Center for the Performing Arts, providing opportunities in the arts for individuals with disabilities. For more information, log onto www.VSAFL.org

Did you borrow this book?

**Now you can have your own copy of
MANATEE MOON**

Send $12.95 ($9.95 plus $3.00 tax, shipping and handling) to:

**AVERY GOODE-REID PUBLISHERS
P.O. BOX 702
ORMOND BEACH, FL   32175-0702**

IS THIS A GIFT? WE'LL BE GLAD TO PERSONALIZE YOUR COPY!

Please allow 2-4 weeks delivery

Or:
**Save yourself the shipping and log onto our web site
www.MarianSTomblin.com for a listing of local retailers.**